THE FALCON
SHIFTER'S HEART
CANDACE COLT

FORWARD

Dear Reader,

Nocturne Falls has become a magical place for so many people, myself included. Over and over I've heard from you that it's a town you'd love to visit and even live in! I can tell you that writing the books is just as much fun for me.

With your enthusiasm for the series in mind – and your many requests for more books – the Nocturne Falls Universe was born. It's a project near and dear to my heart, and one I am very excited about.

I hope these new, guest-authored books will entertain and delight you. And best of all, I hope they allow you to discover some great new authors! (And if you like this book, be sure to check out the rest of the Nocturne Falls Universe offerings.)

For more information about the Nocturne Falls Universe, visit http://www.kristenpainter.com/sugar-skull-books

In the meantime, happy reading!

Kristen Painter

THE FALCON SHIFTER'S HEART
A Nocturne Falls Universe Collection

Copyright © 2017 by Candace Colt

Published in the United States of America.

Cover Design & Formatting by Jaxadora Design
eBook Cover Design by Dreams2Media

FIRST EDITION

Welcome to Nocturne Falls, the town that celebrates Halloween 365 days a year.

The tourists think it's all a show: the vampires, the werewolves, the witches, the occasional gargoyle flying through the sky. But the supernaturals populating the town know better.

Living in Nocturne Falls means being yourself.

Fangs, fur, and all.

A Nocturne Falls Universe Collection

THE FALCON FINDS HIS MATE
THE FALCON TAMES THE PSYCHIC

THE FALCON FINDS HIS MATE

CANDACE COLT

*To my husband who always reminds me when
it's time to get back into the writer's cave.*

THE FALCON FINDS HIS MATE

After her dream job shatters like Humpty's shell, psychic Jess Callahan returns home to Nocturne Falls to put her life back together and get her career back on track. Left heartbroken years ago by a shifter, Jess keeps anything or anyone supernatural at arm's distance; even turning her back on her gift.

His career skyrocketing, falcon shifter Ryan Ford's life is just where he wants it. When the darkly handsome Ryan realizes that the one thing missing from his quiet, stay-to-himself world is the feisty red-haired Jess, he decides she'd be his perfect mate.

When Jess finally opens her heart to Ryan, she also opens her clairvoyant channel. But will their love survive her catastrophic vision?

CONTENTS

CHAPTER ONE

Sipping sweet ice tea from a Mason jar, Jessica 'Jess' Callahan rocked in the porch swing, watching car after car file past; each one packed with gawking tourists dying for Nocturne Falls to open.

"Morning, precious." Echo Stargazer slipped into the seat next to her granddaughter. "Look at that traffic." With the August Reunion Festival kicking off this weekend, cars would be stacked all over town.

"Stacked cars? What a hoot!" Echo said.

Jess slammed her heels on the ground halting the swing. "Nana, you can't keep reading people's thoughts out loud. At least while my friends are here."

"Don't be such a worry wart. They won't arrive until tomorrow. " Echo beamed a crooked grin and waved her knotty-fingered palm. "Decorum, grace, and charm will ooze from my very being."

This would be a supreme challenge for the little lady sitting next to her. "Let's not overdo it," Jess said.

"Moi? Overdo?" Echo slipped a pearl encrusted cuff bracelet from her pocket and polished it on her thigh.

Barefoot in her faded Boston University sleep shirt, Jess marveled at this seventy-six-year-old wearing marigold yellow culottes, a hand-embroidered over-blouse, and full makeup down to crimson lipstick on her wizened lips. Her grandmother had fashionista style.

Sunrise to nightfall, Jess spent the last three months on repairs to their two-story Victorian and applied more color to the walls than her cheekbones.

"You look lovely without makeup," Echo said.

"Thank you, Nana, but don't change the subject. Zoey and Sierra don't know what goes on in this town and no clue about my dear grandmother."

Echo's impish eyes sparkled. "What happens when I'm with clients?"

"Could you meet them somewhere else for the week? How about the Hallowed Bean coffee shop?"

"Where someone's always bellowing orders?"

Echo gestured to the left, and a half-dozen bracelets tinkled down her arm like a wind chime. "A tall Jack O' Lantern Latte with soy, no whip, for Eliza." When she raised her other arm, another half-dozen bangles followed suit. "Double Enchanted Espresso for Jake. In the corner, a card reading for Maude."

"You made your point." Jess opened a weather app on her phone. "Ninety-five by noon."

"Hot enough to fry green tomatoes on the vine. Outstanding. Tourists will flock inside for our cold air conditioning and stay to buy trinkets."

Forever optimistic, Echo's freezer was full of

lemonade squeezed from a lifetime of lemons. She could find a rainbow in a pig sty.

Starting with only five hundred dollars to her name, Echo had leveraged the first floor into the Carpe Diem, a profitable costume and tchotchke shop. Private card readings in their living quarters on the second floor of their carnation pink Victorian home, iced the cake.

As an orphaned eight-year-old, Jess adapted to Nana's quirks. But her college roommates would be here for only a week; not nearly time to adjust to anything.

"Are you finished with the stage?" Echo asked.

Jess shook her head and crunched the last ice cube. Weeks ago, tickets sold out for tomorrow's Ellingham Animal Sanctuary Showcase, the first event of the Reunion Festival. And the Harmswood Academy auditorium stage was far from ready.

Though her stock-and-trade was building elaborate museum displays, she would never again tackle a project like this. Not because she couldn't handle tools—she could.

THE FALCON FINDS HIS MATE

Lassoed into chairing the Showcase, her problems started the moment she called the first work meeting to order. Not that *order* ever reigned. Leading this motley group was a test of wills akin to directing a migrating wildebeest choir.

There'd been more pre-planning, planning-to-plan, and review-the-plan meetings to overflow both claw-footed bathtubs upstairs. Still, they were down to the wire.

Half the volunteers had magical powers; all failed to conjure a break from bad luck. First, the electrical panel blew. The toilets in the women's bathroom wouldn't flush. The AC cashed out. Delivered two days early, three dozen white gladiolus intended for the lobby had drooped and turned brown.

What she wouldn't trade for a day to rest.

"It will go better today, believe me. I talked with the fairies and they agreed to stop their tricks. I told you what would happen if they weren't on your planning committee," Echo said.

"From your mouth to the Goddess's ears." All

Jess wanted was for the show to be over, and to tame her growling stomach with yogurt and fresh Georgia peaches.

"Sliced in the fridge," Echo said.

Jess dropped her chin. Again? "Nana, I love you to tears, but—"

Echo raised a three-finger scout salute. "On my honor…"

The rest lost as a "*meworowow*" and crash rattled the front door.

"I'll get him," Jess said.

Through the threshold sauntered Echo's beloved cat. Focused like a Mini-Sumo wrestler, he faced his opponent, a half-pulverized scratching post. With one paw smack, the contraption succumbed.

Under the cat's stony glower, Jess gathered the broken pieces. "How many does that make?"

"Since you came back? Five, counting this one."

Echo grunted as she lifted a cat the size of a small snowman. "Crealde, honey. Are you sneaking food? Calling pizza delivery after we've gone to bed?"

His purr grew to a lion's roar. Jess covered her ears. "He doesn't like being fat shamed."

"Stop it, Crealde. You'll wake the dead." Echo hooked a thumb over her shoulder to her neighbor's shuttered house. "Though it would take more than a catcall to stir that bunch."

The cat went quiet as Echo's fingers spun over his snow-white fur.

Jess leaned against the wall, arms folded over her chest. "And how do you propose we explain Crealde to houseguests?"

Echo's wide-rimmed glasses magnified her eyes to hockey pucks. "What's to explain?"

Jess gave her temples a deep massage. What's to explain? "Work with me, Nana. Except to us and all supers in Nocturne Falls, your nineteen-pound fur baby with one blue and one green eye is entirely invisible."

"Details. Details. By the way, I've arranged for the Ford brothers to come help today," Echo said.

More *help* meant more novices to herd and Jess didn't have time to play nursemaid.

Wait. Surely she'd heard that wrong.

"Who did you say was coming to help?" Jess craned her neck at an angle toward her grandmother.

"You heard me. Besides, many hands make the load lighter."

For certain, this was a load of something. But not something nice smelling. Jess had managed to steer clear of Connor Ford the whole time she'd been home. It had taken seven years to get over him and ten seconds to jump-start old feelings.

Calm down. This wasn't high school. They weren't kids anymore. He'd probably forgotten all about her as she had him, if only for a minute.

This was so not going to be easy.

While she ate breakfast, Jess couldn't sidestep worry. A dozen times Sierra Everest and Zoey Houston had pestered to come home with her on college breaks. Each time she came up with a baker's dozen reasons against it.

THE FALCON FINDS HIS MATE

Three years after they graduated, she finally caved. Good time as any, Festival week would give them the full Nocturne Falls experience.

She braided her hair and rehearsed ways to explain Nana's eccentricities to Sierra, the world-traveling child of a UN ambassador, and Zoey, a Senator's daughter.

Above all else, explanations had to be simple. Brag on Nocturne Falls, the quaint community that celebrated Halloween all year long. Where diversity was embraced and everyone accepted for who they were.

Coincidences. Echo didn't read thoughts. No magic about it.

Sure. That will work. No problem at all...until the very human Sierra and Zoey saw fangs, fur, or statues that talked, and ran for the hills.

Jess sighed away a long breath. No plausible way around this except the coward's route.

Sneaky as it was, only one thing would work. She would convince Zoey and Sierra to drink the specially charged Nocturne Falls water. Right from the start and often.

Humans who drank Moonbow Water didn't sense any supernatural presence or notice magic. Sad, in a way. There were positive things about being a super, though Jess rarely used her gift.

She rinsed her dishes and glanced out the kitchen window. Nana and Master Cheng were practicing Tai Chi; their dance-like moves synchronized poetry.

No telling how old the man was, or where he lived. Like clockwork, he came every Friday morning, shared time with Nana, and left as quickly as he appeared.

People came and went all the time; in the garden, through the store, and upstairs. Even with privacy at a premium, she was grateful to come home after her dream job shattered like Humpty's shell.

At first, the headhunter called every few days with upbeat prospects. Now Jess's calls went to voicemail. It seemed there weren't many jobs for museum archivists at the moment.

THE FALCON FINDS HIS MATE

She mentally clicked down an unfinished task list. Too little time. The Showcase had to be flawless. No more problems. She could keep Connor and his brother busy in a far corner. Two of the wealthiest men in town helping build a stage? They might not even show up, or be much use if they did.

As she jimmied her work boots over her socks, a sharp thwack heralded brain-searing pain.

What. Just. Happened.

A bent fingernail? She hoped.

She opened one eye at a time. Good news. Not the nail. Bad news. Thumb angled like a U-turn road sign.

Hurts. A lot.

"Noooooo." Crouched on the floor, her head to her knees, she took long slow inhales.

Deep breathing should help. Why didn't it?

CHAPTER TWO

Footsteps. Closer.

"Nana?"

Echo knelt beside Jess. "We heard you all the way downstairs. What on earth is wrong?"

Without raising her head or saying a word, Jess stuck her hand in the air.

"Gracious. I won't even ask how," Echo said.

"Don't." Jess's voice muffled between her knees.

Soft fingers wrapped around her hand, easing the screaming pain to a distant shout. Someone held the wicked renegade thumb.

"I help, Miss." Not Nana's voice. Her eyes

opened a slit to see Master Cheng on his knees beside her. "Hold breath, Miss."

She filled her lungs to capacity and hiked in one more smidgen. Master Cheng clasped her hand and an electrical cavalcade coursed through her.

"Breathe out." The man's hands opened like a delicate lotus blossom. "No more pain."

Jess stared unblinkingly at her perfectly straight thumb.

"No. Not a chance." Ryan Ford's teeth ground at the image in the mirror. Emblazoned across the front of his black T-shirt, in bright shiny letters: I <heart> falcons.

His brother, Connor, wiped workbench sawdust off his hands. "All in the name of charity."

"I don't care if it's for the Queen of Egypt. I wouldn't use this moronic thing to polish wood, let alone wear it. Does Mother realize we're grown men?"

"Always better to humor, than argue with her."

Ryan yanked off the shirt and slapped it over his brother's shoulder. "Fine. *You* wear it. *You* walk across the stage in front of two hundred people."

"Sorry, *bro*." Connor extended the shirt to arms' length. "Mother volunteered you."

"Don't remind me."

Why didn't he just write a check for his appearance, stay here and finish the Fareed project? It hurt to part with the five-foot tall, carved wooden stallion, but the seventy-thousand-dollar commission eased the ache. With the money, he could afford to move his studio off his mother's estate. That day couldn't come soon enough.

"Dude," Connor said. "Mother's crossing the driveway. ETA forty-five seconds. I'm gone."

"If you're determined to abandon me, at least do it on foot and not wing."

Elenora Ellingham, an elder in the Nocturne Falls founding family, forbade shape-shifters to turn during the day. Like that would stop his brother.

Connor flashed a devious grin. "I rise to meet the wind. Later, *bro*." With a finger snap, he shifted into a falcon and took flight out the back door into the woods behind the estate.

"Thanks, *bro*." Ryan stuffed the obnoxious T-shirt into a cabinet seconds before a shadow crossed the threshold, blocking the morning light.

Solange Ford kicked aside wood shavings and walked further into the workshop. "How can you stand this mess?"

How? For starters, to avoid being hassled by a playboy brother and a sharp-tongued mother. Though today solitude was an illusion.

"This is a working studio, Mother. Not a tea room."

"I hoped for a preview of your outfit," Solange said.

He cut a glance to the hiding place where the outlandish shirt would never again see daylight in this lifetime or the next. "Preview or approval?"

"Was that a nice thing to say to your mother?"

Not in the slightest. Ryan remained tight-lipped.

Solange rubbed a hand over her son's cheek

and gave his hair a slight tug. "You could use a shave, and maybe get your hair trimmed, just a teeny bit."

If he could help it, never. "How about I shave my head like Connor?"

"Do not under any circumstance mimic that horrific butchered haircut." His mother went to the door and stared into the pines. "It would mean the world to me if you won."

He ran a cloth down the stallion's smooth haunch. "No matter who wins, the money goes to a good cause."

"But it would be wonderful to boast on my good-looking son."

"Or show off to your cronies?"

In mock displeasure, she rolled her eyes. "Connor is acting so childish. As though I can't see him up there. Has he forgotten who taught you both how to hide? How to wait? And when the moment was right, how to—"

Ryan hammered shut the lid to a tin of wax. "Mother. Don't go there." Hunting prey was in the

Ford DNA, but not something he enjoyed thinking about, nor doing.

After he had mucked up his first, only, and last kill, he became vegetarian.

Solange fluffed her dappled gray hair. "Time to charm your brother from the tree. I believe you're both due at Harmswood."

Modeling in the Showcase was humiliation enough. Building the stage was like forcing condemned men to build their gallows.

And what use would tag along Connor be? It drove Ryan up a wall any time his brother got near a tool.

"One more thing," Solange said.

Always one more thing and the second was never good.

"I found out Jessica Callahan will be there."

Ryan cocked his head toward his mother. "So what?"

"I don't want him tempted into rekindling an old romance."

"Are you kidding? Connor can't remember who

he dated last year. You think he remembers high school?"

"We don't need this now that he's settled down and about to be married."

"The original runaway groom settled down?" His laugh reverberated through the rafters.

Unmoved, Solange faced him. "I've instilled high mating standards in you boys. It doesn't matter how many women you *almost* marry. The one you *do* marry is the one that counts. This union will be an asset. As will yours to Melanie."

Melanie McPherson? That arranged engagement to the highbrow Atlanta shifter had ended a long time ago. Sooner or later, he'd tell his mother, but with the permanent bad mood his she wore like a wetsuit, later worked.

"You never liked Jess or her grandmother because they aren't shifters. Admit it," he said.

"Pfft. Echo Stargazer is a trickster with cheap parlor card games. Even her name is made up. How can you be Evelyn Putnam one day, and become Echo Stargazer the next? And her biggest trick?

THE FALCON FINDS HIS MATE

Passing off that girl as a psychic to get her into Harmswood. The girl has no supernatural powers."

Ryan's blood pressure traveled along a fuse that threatened to blow a hole through his skull. If there were awards for intolerance, his mother would have a full trophy case.

"Nobody gets through the selection procedures by trickery," he said.

Everyone in town loved Echo and nobody cared what she called herself. And humans with magical gifts had the same right to attend Harmswood Academy as any other supernatural.

"So I assume you will help me. That girl burned a hot torch for him." Solange waved over her shoulder. "Ciao."

Who else but his mother would have the unthinking audacity to mention burning torches in this town?

To Ryan's relief, Connor didn't make the trip into town. Inside the bloody hot Harmswood

Academy auditorium, Ryan followed the sounds of hammering and power saws. In a town founded by a family as wealthy as the Ellinghams, why couldn't they spring for a new AC unit?

And what chaos. An ant colony had more purpose. Who was in charge?

Stepping over gaffer-taped audio cables and in between a dozen workers, he tapped the shoulder of a man operating a jig-saw.

"Can you direct me to the supervisor?" Ryan asked.

The man pointed to someone on a ladder on the stage. "Since you're going that way, would you take this?" He handed Ryan a plywood cut-out of some indistinguishable entity.

Turning it in all directions, he couldn't make heads nor tails out of it. Assuming *it* was an animal with a head or tail.

When he reached the ladder, his eyes trailed up a woman's slim blue jean clad legs.

Though he chose to live like a recluse, he still appreciated a nice-looking female, and if this view was any indication, there was much to appreciate.

"Excuse me," he said. But she wore earplugs and didn't hear him.

Since he apparently held a key piece, he waved at her.

Her leather tool belt gently bounced on her curvy hips as she stepped down to join him. She removed her safety goggles and earplugs and offered a tentative smile.

Was that hammering somewhere, or his heart? Glistening in the sweltering room, her creamy skin glowed. "The guy with the saw asked me to bring this," he said.

"The otter. Thank you." She studied him a moment then broke into an engaging smile that burst like spring across her freckled face. "You don't recognize me, do you?"

Her shirt splotched with paint and sawdust. A reversed ball cap. Didn't ring any bells. Wait. Freckles? Scrunched nose when she smiled?

"I'm Jess Callahan."

She had a firm, friendly handshake.

So, this is who his mother assigned him to watch. He made a point of thanking her later. Second thought, he'd keep it to himself.

"I guess you remember me," he said.

"Ryan Ford." She brushed her arms and climbed the ladder, nimbly handling the nail gun to attach the mystery piece.

She rejoined him and crossed her arms under her ample breasts. "It looks a little rough. Paint will make all the difference."

Nothing about her looked rough. But he couldn't say the same for that mismatched shape conglomeration.

He tilted his head from side-to-side. "I still can't make out an otter." Or any other natural animal in the universe.

Her back stiffened. Not promising.

He tried another tact. "White clouds and blue sky?"

Was he imagining superheated daggers flying from her half-closed eyelids?

"Excuse me, but the Harmswood art club

designed this stage." Her words measured through gritted teeth, she looked like someone about to shift to a very agitated animal.

CHAPTER THREE

Swift move, Ford. The advantage to hibernating in his studio was that wooden sculptures didn't care what he said or how he said it. But people, on the other hand, did.

"That didn't come out right," he said.

"The kids worked hard on this design. And I happen to like it."

Anger didn't look good on many women, but on this redhead, it weaved cute with sexy.

"It was a stupid thing to say from someone who just walked in the door. I came to help, so put me to work," he said.

Her face softened, though her still flushed

cheeks matched her ginger hair.

"You can finish the side sections." She unfolded a sketch sheet and smoothed it against the wall.

In seconds, he committed the design to memory. He let her keep talking to listen to her lilting voice. Standing this close, he caught her light fragrance. Roses.

She refolded the paper and put it in her pocket. "You ever use a table saw?"

He swallowed his amusement. His love affair with woodworking started in second grade. This was no challenge.

"I have."

"Holler if you need help," she said.

He chose some sturdy plywood from a pile and set to work. In less than forty-five minutes, he measured, cut, made a few embellishments and assembled the pieces.

Jess came up behind him. "You did all this by yourself?"

"Seems I did." From the moment he started any

project, time boundaries vanished. Hours and meals passed when he was in the zone.

While Jess fastened the sections on the stage, he held them for her and stole more than one look at her toned arms and firm full breasts. What had happened to the gawky little kid?

"Could hold still? We could get this done a lot faster if you'd pay attention," she said.

Oh, he was paying attention all right. Not to the boards. "Sorry." But not for staring.

Facepalm moment. Which one was the mind reader? Jess or her grandmother? Damned if he remembered. He kept his mouth shut and his thoughts in check.

The aroma of grilled onions and peppers coming from a food truck outside sent his stomach into a happy dance.

This woman didn't seem to be a threat, nullifying any obligation to his mother. Nor did he intend to miss a chance to spend time with this fine-looking woman. He just hoped Connor stayed away. Far away. Amazon jungle away.

THE FALCON FINDS HIS MATE

He cleared a nervous throat tickle. "Join me for lunch? My treat."

Bent over, she ran her fingers through her unbraided hair that streamed like silk. Jess cocked her head toward him and squinched her eyes into a curious stare.

Had he sprouted wings? He flexed his arms and fingers. Fully human.

Still bent upside down, Jess's face lit up, and to his amazement, she righted herself and accepted his invitation.

Dodging workers installing lights in tree branches over an outdoor patio, they found seats at a picnic table. Though the midday sun was as hot as a convection oven, their shaded spot was still cooler than the auditorium.

"Wonder why we haven't run into each other before today?" Ryan asked.

She wiped a sweat bead from her cleavage. "Unless you're a regular shopper at the DIY Depot, you probably wouldn't."

The Harmswood class change bell reverberated

across the campus, bringing small talk to a jarring end.

Jess covered her ears until it stopped. "Guess they don't turn it off for the summer. Can you believe how many times a day that thing rang? Start class. End class. Lunch break. Go home. We marched around like baby ducks."

The only good things about Harmswood were wood shop and art class. Everything else was a distant blur. Including Jess.

Two classes ahead, Ryan only remembered that she was a nice kid, but not a standout. Nothing like this beauty, who along with the whole Harmswood female teenage population, had a crush on Connor.

"How long are you staying in Nocturne Falls?" He watched the growing onion pile Jess picked off her meatball sub. Excellent to add to his grilled Portobello but how would it look to ask someone he barely knew for her spare onions?

"I was roadkill from a downsized museum. My headhunter thinks I'll have a job by October." She pushed her plate toward him. "Help yourself."

"Oh, no. I'm sorry. I couldn't." Perhaps this *was* the mind reader.

"Go ahead. You're eyeing them like a hawk." She covered her mouth. "I didn't just say hawk."

Ryan shrugged as he scooped the onions. "Common mistake. Most people can't tell a hawk from a falcon."

"Well, I can." She wiped away laughter tears. "It was a slip of the tongue."

A sense of humor after all. Keeping tabs on this woman might be easier than he thought. His day had just brightened like a second sunrise.

Jess looked around again, at least the fifth time in the last twenty minutes. "Everything okay?" He asked.

"I thought Connor was supposed to be here."

Exit sunrise; enter sunset.

CHAPTER FOUR

"Wait." "Don't lock us in."

Swathed in a high-end perfume cloud, three women raced downstairs and sped past as Jess told the part-time sales clerks goodnight and started to set the Carpe Diem night alarm.

Another of her grandmother's group rate sessions. Echo's talent for marketing matched her knack with the cards.

Upstairs, Jess took a seat at a large table draped with a fringed floral cloth. Clients either left this table in tears or overjoyed. The little ensemble that had scurried out fit the latter. "It went well; I take it."

THE FALCON FINDS HIS MATE

"I shouldn't do so many readings in a row. I'm exhausted," Echo said.

Jess took off her work boots and massaged her feet. "I can relate to that."

Next to Echo's wooden card box, smoky sage wisps rose from an abalone shell, slipping into every crevice of Jess's memory.

The world was right and grounded when her grandmother burned sage.

"Did your extra workers show up?" Echo asked.

"Yes." And no.

Ryan Ford had been a pleasant surprise. Somehow he'd outgrown his gothy-nerd phase and turned into a nice-looking guy.

Not his fault that she'd been distracted at lunch. She'd jockeyed nervousness about seeing Connor, with disappointment that he never made an appearance.

Echo moved a philodendron plant from the antique pie chest and set it in the middle of the table; then she sat in a high-backed chair that didn't match the other three, or anything else in the house.

"How's your thumb?" Echo asked.

Jess hadn't given it a thought since this morning. "Someday tell me how he did that."

"Simple. He moved Chi."

Naturally. Why had she even asked? Everyone can move Chi. Nana's mysterious friends.

To give her grandmother more room, Jess pulled on the table, which didn't move a millimeter. Gripping the table edge, she gave it another full heave. Still to no avail other than raising a howl from below that rattled heaven's gates. The leg hadn't caught the rug.

Crealde strolled out and fired a death ray scowl from his mismatched eyes. He plopped in the middle of the room and gave his shoulder an annoyed grooming.

Which side of Alice's mushroom had Jess bitten? Had she outgrown the house, or was the house closing in on her?

Echo once followed a rule that for each thing

that came in, two went out. That had worked for a week, ten years ago.

"Hoarder" didn't describe Echo. A kinder term was "rescuer." She adopted things. Lamps, chests, chairs, paintings, or objects d'art. There was room in this house for anything if it was frilly, pastel, chintz, shabby and chic.

Echo brushed spilled ashes into the shell. "Before I put these cards away, would you like a reading? On the house." Echo's giggle tinkled like a spoon against bone china.

Jess pressed her sweaty hands into her knees. Not because she didn't believe in the cards or her grandmother's clairsentience. She did. Both her parents had gifts. But what good were they? Nothing prevented them from dying.

The summer after she came to live with her grandmother, Jess's clairvoyance emerged. Without mentors at Harmswood and her grandmother's wisdom, the magical gift could easily have become a curse.

"This is your shtick, Nana. Not mine. All I

want is something to eat, a long soaking bath, and then dissolve into sleep."

Echo shuffled the cards and set the deck on the table. "You don't have to if you aren't sure."

Never sure; always curious. And her grandmother wouldn't budge until she went through with this.

"One and done," Jess said.

"Set your intention," Echo said. "You can keep the ring on. The cards can't be blocked."

Not reassuring. Passed down from Jess's mother, the jade ring blocked all clairvoyant visions.

She kept it on. Always.

On the other side of exhaustion, she doubted the cards cared that sleep was her primary intention.

She opted for a general, easy-peasy, open-ended reading. Let the cards talk to her if they so choose. Otherwise, goodnight and off to bed.

Though it had been years, she remembered the ritual.

Right hand over her heart, feeling each beat's

sharp thump, Jess spread the deck in an arc with her left hand.

Each glossy black card was identical. After a long minute, she pulled one that shimmered.

"Keep your awareness on the card. Observe. Don't judge. Be present right here." Echo dropped her chin to her chest and shut her eyes. "Now we wait."

Jess tapped her toes against the table leg to stay awake. When that didn't help, she scooted in the chair, scrunching the tablecloth in her hands.

A sudden chill dusted her skin from scalp to toes.

The chill.

Nana's go-to method to get her little granddaughter to behave. No timeouts. No second warnings. Grownup Jess rubbed her arms hoping to erase the gooseflesh.

"Be present or it won't work," Echo warned. "And stop fidgeting."

Okay. One more try. Jess closed her eyes. In seconds, she popped them open as something brushed her cheek.

A bright, translucent orb glided past her face then hovered over her card. Jess gasped as it burst like a soap bubble, raining mist over the table.

Good thing she trusted her grandmother as this verged on creepy. She should be used to strange things happening in this house, but her racing heart was not.

The image on the card sharpened and turned her inside out.

Echo leaned forward. "You saw something. It shows all over your face."

"Nothing. I must be too tired." She shoved the card into the deck, crazy to play this game in the first place.

"What was it? Tell me."

Jess opened her mouth to answer, but the words tumbled into her stomach.

Clear as crystal, an image had seared her brain.

Drawn curtains in a dark room. A faint trace of patchouli. Something sat on a pristine bed. Her grandmother's bedroom, but no Nana.

CHAPTER FIVE

Jess darted like a nervous rabbit as she ran errands downtown.

Yesterday's image on Nana's card put her stress in a stranglehold.

What did it mean? A warning? A premonition? Or, guilt?

From the first day, she knew her grandmother had trouble taking care of Carpe Diem. Keeping busy with repairs smothered denial. Until now.

How long until she had the hard talk with her Nana about giving up the Carpe Diem? Then what would become of Echo Stargazer?

Jess had considered staying in town, but there

was nothing left here. Childhood friends had either moved away or married with families. So many new faces.

Lifelong story; she didn't fit in anywhere.

One last stop at Delaney's Delectables for fresh bread for dinner and Scary Scream Scones for breakfast.

"Excited about judging tonight?" Delaney Ellingham, the owner and proprietor, asked.

Excited? Umm. Not quite. "We're sold out."

"That's wonderful news. Our family will be delighted. I even convinced my husband to come to the after party. It's so hard to get him out of the house."

Make that doubly hard for Jess. Despite Zoey's and Sierra's efforts to convert her into a party connoisseur, she would rather stay home and watch how-to videos. Anything other than socializing with strangers.

Those two women held their own anywhere, but a gymnasium half full of dancing supers might create a little situation.

THE FALCON FINDS HIS MATE

One more thing to add to her shopping list; Nocturne Falls bottled water.

The last stop would be the Hallowed Bean for a coffee. In a rush and juggling the bakery bag and her drink, she scarcely noticed that someone held the door.

With an automatic 'thank you' nod, she didn't make eye contact with her benefactor.

"Jess Callahan. That you?"

A vaguely familiar voice. She stepped aside for a tourist family dressed as skeletons to pass, then looked at the person still holding the door.

A shiny, Vin Diesel bald head; buffed arms like mortar cannons, and that same full-of-himself smirk that every Harmswood female, including her, had adored.

Connor Ford.

Her stomach dropped like granite.

In school, he'd carried himself like a GQ model. Today he'd qualify for 'Muscle Man Monthly.' This Connor looked like a guy who never met a mirror he didn't like.

With him was Ryan in a wrinkled denim shirt, tousled brown hair, and a days-old beard. He looked a bit scruffy but, she reminded herself, he had been a tremendous help.

Who would ever guess these two were brothers?

She locked on Ryan's brown eyes. "Hello, again."

Ryan responded with a cautious smile. "Good to see you." His low, deep voice caused an unfamiliar stirring in her chest that she couldn't blame on her untouched caffeine. Timeout. She had to harness this runaway horse.

Connor pointed to a small café table. "Will you join us?"

Shielding against rapid fire nerves, she dodged eye contact with either brother. "I really should go. Million things to do." So why didn't her legs take the hint?

"Five minutes? Ryan, snag our drinks. I'll wait here," Connor said.

Ryan rolled his eyes. "Sure. Love to, *bro*. Let

THE FALCON FINDS HIS MATE

me know if there's anything else I can do for you." Connor waved his hand toward a scowling Ryan.

She guessed she could spare five minutes, even if she'd stepped into something between these two. Her metal chair grated over the concrete and vibrated through every bone in her body.

Or was this her body sending caution signals?

Connor slumped half-horizontal in his chair, legs spread like a cocky high school quarterback. Fine for a seventeen-year-old. But Connor was twenty-six.

Jess sat tall and erect. Had she spent years on a crippling puppy love for this guy?

"So how've you been?" Connor asked.

What had she expected? 'I've been empty since the day I dumped you like a potato sack.'

Bull crap.

She could lie. Say her career had taken a meteoric rise. With more money than she knew what to do with, she was passing through on a visit.

But Ryan probably already told him everything.

"Fine." Mighty impressive answer. "I

understand you're getting married."

"Yes." Connor's voice dropped. He looked inside for his brother. "How long does it take to get coffee?"

"Is the lucky bride from here?"

He shook his head. "North Carolina."

"A shifter?"

"Falcon like us," he said in an unenthusiastic murmur. "So is Ryan's fiancé."

Fiancé? Funny how that never came up yesterday. But, why would it? Two people sitting across from each other at a table didn't mean a real date.

Of course, the Ford brothers chose falcon-shifter mates. Solange Ford must be over the moon. Even for a minute, she'd never accepted that her son might have an interest in a non-shifter. Though Connor's *interest* had been debatable, it had served to torque Solange.

Ryan returned and handed his brother a cup. "Too long to stand in line for overpriced coffee. You owe me."

THE FALCON FINDS HIS MATE

"Next time," Connor said.

"This *was* the next time," Ryan said.

The Fords were among the richest in town, and these two clowns were playing price ping pong? These guys were something else.

The drink's heat had diminished in direct proportion to her lost patience and she was ready to split.

Life was too short to babysit bickering brothers. How handy to shift into a bird and fly away right now. Better yet, why didn't *they*?

"Well, guess I'll see you tonight." She gathered her packages and disappeared into the crowd.

Ryan tapped his cup while keeping an eye on Jess.

Who blamed her for leaving after the asinine rant about coffee prices? Had the woman even spoken ten words?

Their mother didn't need to worry about anybody holding torches for either Ford.

"Happy with yourself?" Ryan asked.

Conner shook his head in bewilderment. "What did I do?"

As far as Ryan remembered, Connor hadn't done anything consequential. But this time he had. "You ran her away." He spun the cup Jess left behind.

"She's sure a little hottie. Wonder if she's dating anyone?" Connor asked.

"Did you forget you're getting married in two months?"

"And?"

Ryan fisted his hands, disgusted at the lustful look in his brother's eyes. "Leave her alone. She's a nice kid."

"That, my brother, was no kid."

"Stay away from her."

Connor rocked his chair on two legs. "I told her you were engaged."

Consumed by anger, Ryan fought the urge to punch the smirk from Connor's face. "Why'd you do that? It's not true."

"In mother's world, officially, you are. Don't you think you should break the news to her?"

"That is none of your business."

"Really? And nosing into my business is yours?"

When it came to Jess Callahan, it damn well was.

CHAPTER SIX

"Your grandmother is adorable." Sierra Everest said. "And your house is out of this world."

As were most things in Nocturne Falls. Jess muted a laugh.

Zoey Houston never stopped scanning the dining room. "I've seen vintage houses, but nothing like this. Are those the original chandelier crystals?"

"Trust me, they are. I washed every single one. Speaking of water, I apologize for the heat. We're in a drought." Jess pushed unopened water bottles closer to her friends. "I'm big on hydration."

"I'm floating. We drank water the whole drive from the Atlanta airport," Zoey said.

Sierra took a bottle and read the label. "Moonbow Water? That's so clever."

Jess's hopes rose, then crashed when Sierra put it down.

"Tonight's a costume event, and I don't have a thing. Aren't there clothes downstairs?" Zoey asked.

As they spun through the Carpe Diem costume racks, Sierra and Zoey alternated nods of approval or vetoes.

Sierra held up an adult's princess dress and quickly put it back on the rack. "So what's this contest your grandmother was talking about?"

Jess picked at a non-existent spot on her leg. "It's a charity Showcase."

Zoey shook her head at another offer of water. "A talent thing?"

In a way. Jess sifted for the right words in her brain-o-dex. "Call it a fashion show."

Sierra perked up. "Fashion?"

"Not what you might think." Come on, don't dodge this one. These are smart women. Too bad they weren't thirsty ones.

"The contestants will show animals from the local Sanctuary. They'll be judged on how well their costumes complement the animal they'll be showing." Jess wondered if this made any sense.

The girls nodded that they understood, though that was unlikely.

"So these contestants are locals?" Zoey asked.

"Right." Jess bit her tongue. Explaining that the contestants were the human form of their shifted animal might be a little much.

"Any available men going to be there?" Sierra asked.

That question was bound to come, sooner or later. But, an hour and a half after they arrived?

"I'm sure you'll get an eyeful. There are plenty eligible men in town," Jess said.

Some even human.

"Over your fit?" Connor hefted up on a workbench.

THE FALCON FINDS HIS MATE

Dogged by his brother, Ryan had retreated to his workshop after the disaster at the Hallowed Bean.

He wiped his hands on a rag and ran a critical eye over the wooden horse. "Don't you have anything to do besides harass me?"

"Not really. The joy of being filthy rich. Nowhere to be. Nothing to do. "

Ryan loathed doing *nothing* as much as his brother reveled in it. "Well, I'm on a deadline. She ships in a week," he said.

"This is the best thing you've done yet."

A shocking glimmer of rare sincerity. "That sounded like a compliment. I hope the Fareeds love it as much as I do," Ryan said.

"Why wouldn't they? How are you getting it there?"

"Their family jet."

"You freaking kidding me? Why don't you ride along?"

"They invited me." And he hadn't refused, yet.

"I'd go in a minute." Connor slid down from

the counter. "Look, I was over the line about you and Melanie. But if Mother hears the news from someone else first, you'll be disowned. Not all bad, come to think. Then maybe she'll move me to number one son."

"Sorry you can't stay, *bro*. You *flying* or driving to Harmswood tonight?"

"I'll drive. Can't tell how the evening will end. Been awhile since I dated a redhead. Ciao."

Ciao. That pretentious word again. Like talons down a blackboard.

Connor went through women like a spoiled kid who ignored week-old toys. His next plaything would not be Jess Callahan.

Nothing left to do on the stallion. He knew it. The truth was, he'd didn't want to part with it. One last time he went to the sculpture.

"Friend, if you could run free, what would you do first?" He stood in silence as though the two-hundred-pound hunk of wood could answer.

"We're ready," Jess called from the bedroom.

"Wait for the music," Echo said.

Seconds later Vivaldi's 'Four Seasons' resounded throughout the old Victorian home. Zoey and Sierra cast sideways glances, amusing Jess.

"Let's just say my grandmother does everything with flourish."

"Ladies, you may begin," Echo proclaimed.

"Sierra, you first. And the more theater, the better. Nana loves it."

Jess announced, "May it please your majesty, your first visitor is Salty Sierra."

"Seriously? The best you could come up with?" Sierra murmured.

They looked at each other and giggled.

"Just work it," Jess said.

Salty Sierra, her chest poured into a leather bustier, swaggered from the bedroom. At five foot eight, and thigh-high stiletto boots, she towered over her friends.

In her magenta skirt slit from her hip to the South Pole, Salty Sierra removed her tri-corner hat and bowed. Her curly black hair fell to her shoulders in a messy tangle. "My queen, I've been at sea twenty months and claimed a hundred islands in your name."

Echo offered her hand, and Sierra made a grand gesture to kiss one of the many rings that adorned the old woman's fingers. "Rise my dear and take your place beside me. And who's next?" Echo's voice sang.

"The cat goddess, Bast," Jess said.

It took an hour to get the eyes right, but after laughing through the afternoon, the elaborate kohl artwork had channeled down Bast's cheek. They had decided to call the new look zombie meets cat woman.

To heighten the effect, Zoey borrowed Jess's favorite gold dress. "If you don't sit down, you'll be fine," Jess warned.

"Not sure how I'll manage this all night." Zoey wiggled the tight-fitting dress over her hips. "Oh, my staff."

Zoey made a quick turn to the bedroom and

retrieved the wooden spoon they'd sprayed and glittered, then stood in the dining room doorway. "May I approach?"

"Come forward," Echo said.

"Greetings from the Nile." Zoey made a skirt-hike prevention bow.

"You are most welcome here. Where is my last visitor?"

Jess ran her hands down her sleeveless crocheted smock layered over a beige hemp jumper. Shiny work boots completed her outfit.

Sierra had styled Jess's hair in relaxed braids. Platinum gray shadowed her brown eyes, and crimson cherry lipstick glazed her lips.

Echo embraced her granddaughter and adjusted the floppy silk flower clipped in Jess's hair. "You look magnificent." She gathered all three girls into a hug. "You're all magnificent. I love you all."

Zoey fanned with the spoon. "I sure hope wherever we're going is air conditioned."

"How about some cool water?" Jess prayed they'd drink at least a little bit before the show.

Soon, they'd be seeing Nocturne's best-looking shapeshifters parade across the stage.

Make that a lot of water.

"Still no luck?" Echo whispered.

"Nope. They haven't touched a drop. Where's Crealde?"

"Sleeping on my bed."

Relieved, Jess rejoined her friends. What was wrong with Sierra? Her lips were swelled like bee stings. Allergic reaction?

"What's going on with your mouth?"

Sierra's stretched lips grew to a wide-open, jaw-cracking smile, revealing fake vampire teeth.

Jess groaned. If her vamp friends saw this.

"Honey, they've seen worse." Echo said.

Jess closed her eyes. "Where's your bracelet?" Her Nana had promised.

Echo raised her hand. "Wearing it all along. Sometimes it's a lucky guess." She clapped to get the girls' attention. "I have an announcement. I've arranged for a driver."

Driver? Which one of her grandmother's

friends would that be? "It's not necessary. I'll take us."

"A chauffeur? I love it," Zoey said.

"This is so awesome." Sierra pulled her phone from her bustier. "Photos. Photos. Photos. Downstairs to the porch."

Echo tapped a number into her jewel-encrusted cell phone. "Darling, can you bring the car? Splendid."

Jess opened a bottled water and gulped it down. What other little tricks did her Nana have hiding in her culottes?

CHAPTER SEVEN

Salty Sierra and Bast took selfies downstairs while Jess stayed behind, perspiration flowering under her arms.

"We do not need a chauffeur," she said, each word measured with alchemist precision.

Echo steadied on Jess's elbow as they walked down the stairs. "You're my granddaughter and a prestigious contest judge. This is a big deal. You must arrive in style."

The big deal would be when this was over and done. "I'm pretty sure who you called won't get any votes for safe-driver."

"Because someone's departed doesn't mean

they have forgotten how to drive. If that were true, a third of this town would sell their cars." Echo cackled. "Get it?"

She got it all right; though it was true. Maybe Nocturne Falls would be safer with fewer immortals behind the wheel, but Echo missed the point.

"Relax, precious. Making sure people have happy memories is the most important thing you can do. It's how I hope I'm remembered."

"Does scaring them senseless with a ghost driver equal happiness?"

"Do they act scared?"

Sierra and Zoey took more photos, this time beside the 1955 pink Fleetwood Cadillac in the driveway. And dressed in a white jumpsuit, Elvis posed with them.

"No, but I sure wish they'd drink water." Jess pointed her jade-ringed index finger. "This one time, Nana. No more surprises while they're here. You have to promise."

"Deal. Now go. Have fun."

Jess wrapped her arms around Echo who

seemed to be growing tinier each day. "I wish you were coming with us."

"I'm getting into my PJs, finishing my lemon ginger cookies with a pot of tea, and watching "Charmed" season four CD."

When the last sunset hues waned, Nocturne Falls' streetlights turned the town into a playful nighttime fairyland.

"I can't believe it," Zoey said as Elvis drove down Main Street. "Is it always decorated for Halloween?"

"Yes, ma'am," Elvis said in a slow Southern drawl.

"And everyone wears costumes?" Sierra asked.

Jess smoothed her skirt. "The people in costumes are tourists." Most of the time.

Zoey and Sierra spun around shooting video.

"So, Elvis," Sierra said. "Where's the best nightlife around here?"

His dark eyes sent a silent question to Jess who

gave a tiny, quick headshake. The best club in town was Insomnia.

No law prevented humans from going to this off-the-grid spot for supers if they were with a member.

But, there might not be enough Moonbow Water on the planet to keep Zoey and Sierra from going into shock at what they'd see inside.

Think fast. These were two world-class partiers who didn't think a whit about staying out all night. By their standards tame, but on short notice this might work.

"I bet I forgot to tell you about the after party."

Elvis waved as he drove away. "That was the best impersonator, ever. Even a spot-on accent."

"Uh huh," Jess said. Spot-on indeed.

"He must make a fortune at parties." Zoey tied her white souvenir scarf around her neck. "And handing these out was brilliant. Does he have an act around here?"

"Not so much anymore. You could say he's

retired." Change the subject. "I'll be with the other judges. Your seats are on the first row behind me."

"Will Elvis be at the party?" Zoey wiggled the dress over her hips for the umpteenth time. "He's kinda cute."

Pretending not to hear, Jess waved at and talked to, anyone she could. "Great Frankenstein's monster." "Love your Dracula cape." "You look just like a zombie."

She pressed through the noisy crowd, settled her friends into their seats, and went backstage for final instructions.

Once the judges took their places, Elenora Ellingham stepped to the microphone, thanked everyone for their support, and explained the contest.

Winners would be selected based on confidence displayed in handling their animal, and their creative incorporation of animal traits in their attire. The judges' votes would be averaged with audience votes sent to #nocturnecharity.

Elenora asked Jess to stand as the curtain

opened. Lighting transformed the plywood stage into an enchanted forest, better than Jess ever hoped. Goosebumps covered her as the crowd erupted in applause.

She scanned the audience hoping to give Ryan a thumbs-up for all his help. Instead, she locked eyes on the one scowling face in the whole crowd, Solange Ford.

With a female falcon perched on his leather glove, Ryan stood in the impromptu green room and adjusted the bird's hood. Around him were two dozen other Nocturne Falls shifters, each with an animal. This thing better start soon or the show would take a completely different turn.

"I need to take him out," the wolf handler said.

"Make it quick. You're fourth." Impatient, the stage manager scrolled through her computer tablet. "People. Time to line up. Where's the cougar?"

A breathless woman in a skintight taupe leather jumpsuit slipped into the room. "Here." Her big cat strained the leash.

"Calm your animal, madam." The stage manager continued roll call. Fox, eagle, crow, baby black bear, lynx, owl, boa constrictor, and on down the list.

"Where's the coyote?" Frazzled, the stage manager called again. "Where are they? We start in five minutes. "

That woman's shrill voice could split a hundred-year-old oak down the middle and did nothing to settle the animals. "They dropped out," Ryan said.

"I wish someone had told me. Mr. Ford, you'll take their place."

Though this falcon was used to crowds, this was a new environment. He sensed the animal's agitation, though she was much better with the coyote gone.

Amused, he remembered how Elenora had wrapped an admonishment around her contestant reminders after the coyote's hasty exit. 'We simply cannot have an Ellingham event ruined by a chaotic predator and prey Armageddon. You must control your animals."

The royal 'we.' She and his mother had been carved from the same branch.

He still wished Connor had taken this gig. His brother was the showman; the guy who always wanted center stage. The party boy. All those traits Ryan didn't have or want.

But, he loved how the Ellingham's supported the Sanctuary. That made this never-ending wait tolerable. All the animals were getting restless, and the oblivious damn woman with the pacing cat was no help.

The falcon relaxed as Ryan smoothed the bird's feathers and cooed to it. Except for cat woman, the remaining shifter-handlers knew how to settle their animals.

Trite, yet never truer; it takes one to know one.

When he heard the crowd applaud Jess Callahan, pride poured over him. She deserved every accolade.

What was his mother's big deal? Jess left seven

years ago. Nobody 'carries a torch' for anyone that long. He pitied any girl who carried one for Connor with two almost-weddings down, one on the tarmac.

His falcon's talons tightened around the leather glove. "Sorry, girl." He placed his hand on the bird.

If someone would just lay a reassuring hand on him. Eating a bowl of sawdust sounded better than walking out on that stage.

After what seemed an interminable delay, the stage manager motioned him to step forward. "Ford and the falcon. Next."

From the stage wing, he made out a few faces. His mother sat with her little clique and Connor was nowhere to be seen.

No wonder his mother looked like she'd swallowed a turpentine martini. In the middle of the judges' row sat Jess Callahan.

After the nonsense at the coffee shop, he probably put a lock on the last place on her ballot. Despite that, with Jess and his mother in the same room, this event had jettisoned to new heights. Before the night ended, he might witness a

THE FALCON FINDS HIS MATE

Shakespearean tragedy.

As his name was announced, he spoke softly to the falcon. "Let's rock this place."

CHAPTER EIGHT

"Our next contestant has a three-year-old Kestrel falcon. This fully-grown female is an extraordinary ambassador for the Sanctuary. Her handler is a life-long Nocturne Falls resident, Mr. Ryan Ford."

Jess's stomach danced a two-step. Why didn't he tell her? She whipped through papers in her judge binder. Nowhere were the handlers identified; only the animals.

Well, duh. Who else would show a falcon?

In an admirable faked calm, she leaned into her creaky metal chair. Snagged on her smock, the binder jerked toward her and tipped on the table at a precarious angle. The slap to stop it jettisoned her pen into her lap.

Reorganizing, she mouthed apologies to the other judges and Elenora. Would anyone miss her if she dove under the table's modesty drapes?

Wits and judge's demeanor gathered, she focused on Ryan's exceptional outfit. Gray, blue, and rust colored appliqued feathers interwove over the shoulders of his tweed jacket. His untucked black dress shirt hugged his torso. A mischievous lock of hair dangled over his eyes. And he'd shaved?

Had this sexy man been hiding inside Ryan all along? She wiped her hand across her forehead. Did the air conditioner quit again?

Hand shaking, she marked her ballot then gave him a sideways peek.

Words bounced around in her head. Irresistible. Attractive. Hot.

Engaged.

As he left the stage, Jess watched as the falcon closed her talons around Ryan's glove.

He turned once more to her. Is this what a falcon's prey feels just before the capture?

Dazed by her muddled feelings, after the Showcase ended Jess wound through the crowd on their way to the after party. Zoey detoured into the middle of handlers and animals standing next to the transport vans.

Inside the gym, Zoey caught up with Jess and Sierra. "These creatures are gorgeous," Zoey said.

"Speaking of gorgeous. Whew! Howdy Doo, the man with the falcon is way past good looking." Sierra had sidled up to them as they walked into the packed gym. "Those delicious chocolatey bedroom eyes were on you the whole time. You two got a thing?"

"I went to school with his brother." Jess fanned her skirt over her knees. Was anyone else in here smothering?

"That red face says there's more," Sierra said.

Jess spotted a galvanized tub full of ice and bottled drinks. "Just a minute."

Mustering restraint from jumping fully dressed

into the ice water, she opened a lemonade letting the cool liquid quench her thirst. Time to regroup.

What flipped the switch from seeing Ryan as a nice guy to what spun in her heart?

The jacket and black shirt that embraced him like a second skin? His sharp, dark eyes that cut through her as though she was the only woman in the room?

Or had it been an act to win her vote?

Among the most desirable men in Nocturne Falls, the Fords were in a different league. They were shifters from a wealthy family and lived in the Wolf Creek gated community on the other side of town; well beyond Jess's world.

Making sure no one watched, she slipped an ice cube down her dress.

"I'd ice down, too, if I had a man like that staring at me," Sierra said.

Jess widened her eyes and stiffened. "Who's staring?"

"Like you can't tell." Sierra stirred her hand around the drink tub and took a fruit punch. "The falcon guy."

Shivers rippled over Jess. Was 'falcon guy' gawking at her through the whole ice cube cool down?

"He's coming this way," Sierra said.

"Stop messing with me. Why on earth would he—"

"Evening, ladies." A deep voice cut through the crowd noise and over the band.

"Well, hello there." With a smile wider than a six-lane highway, Sierra extended her hand. "I'm Sierra Everest. Jess has told me so much about you. Gotta run, but I hope to see you again. Soon."

Sierra's Cheshire grin lingered as she slipped beyond Jess's grasp. Good thing.

Clearing her throat, Jess summoned her perky voice. "Sorry, you didn't win."

Ryan shook his head. "Not a problem for me. But Mother's fit to be tied. I'm sure the Cougar won by a landslide. The handler's costume was, well, seductive."

Jess pursed her lips to hold a giggle at how

Ryan's face had blushed. Coming from Mr. Conservative, 'seductive' sounded almost charming.

He looked to each side and leaned toward her. "Do your friends know about us?"

The death grip she held on the plastic bottled resulted in an embarrassing high-pitched crackle. "What about us?"

His gentle laugh that mingled with his clove and forest pine aftershave percolated some un-innocent notions of 'us.'

"Our nether-side," he said.

Oh, that. Not us-as-a-couple, though for a fleeting second, that sounded good. Hold it. The guy has a fiancé.

And she knew better than to reveal supernaturals' true nature to casual visitors.

"What makes you think I mentioned you?" That came out all wrong. And Sierra had already told the big lie that she had. "I mean; I don't talk about men with them." Nobody would believe that. Time to shut her mouth and stay out of this sinkhole.

She scanned the room and realized there were

more supers in here than humans. And two humans better get to drinking some water.

The super standing next to her straightened tall. Very tall. Her eyes scanned up Ryan's chest to his face, all smiles as he—oh no—*stared* at her. Even if the world chanted 'om' right this minute, her body wouldn't take the calming hint.

"Hello, beautiful." A raspy voice buzzed in her ear.

Jess's reverie door slammed shut.

Ryan's face went rock hard and reinforced her hunch; things were about to get interesting.

CHAPTER NINE

Once Jess would have traded her left pinkie for Connor Ford's arm around her. After all this time, it felt wrong.

"I can't keep my eyes off you, Your Judgeship." Connor gave her another tug. "Heard you lost, *bro*. That little cougar had you by a mile. So, Judge Jess, let's catch some fresh air."

"Too *stuffy* in here for you, *bro*?" Ryan asked.

Squirming from Connor's grip, Jess could see Ryan's growing fury. Standing between two livid falcons was not smart.

She arced her finger in Connor's direction. "When did this become a 'let's go' moment?"

"My bad." Connor waved at someone across the room. "I'll grab drinks and meet you in the courtyard." He gave her a quick kiss on the cheek.

Faster than she could process, instinct drew her hand to where his lips had touched her skin. Not sensual or loving; a quick peck. Nonetheless, a kiss.

"I'm not sure what just happened," she said.

Ryan snuffed an indignant snicker. "My brother. That's what. You'd never guess he's getting married soon."

His expression was more than a few notches below joyful. He directed his dark eyes into hers with the same intent focus he'd had on stage.

"Be careful," he said.

"Of what?"

"Him."

College and working in Boston taught her how to handle men a lot worse than Connor.

Though he had one little trait the others didn't have; half falcon.

"He's a presumptuous jerk," she hissed, forgetting she was talking about Ryan's brother.

"Sorry."

"That's a kind way to describe him. I'll remember that one."

He hooked the tweed jacket over his shoulder. Perspiration had sealed his shirt to his broad, muscular torso.

A long inhale quieted her heartbeat. He wouldn't be showing off on purpose, would he? Hardly. Not this guy.

A young girl shoved between them. "Can I have your picture, Mr. Ford? I have two tickets."

Tickets. Yes. Her brilliant plan to raise money with handler photos. She'd had no inkling Ryan would be the center of teenage infatuation.

"Jess, would you mind holding my jacket?"

Ryan rolled up his sleeves; an unwitting invitation to the entire female population in the gym.

The first girl was followed by two, three, a dozen. Young girls, women in their twenties, even older, lined up and waved raffle tickets.

With no clue how elegant he looked, Ryan

graciously allowed each one to have a turn, even holding their camera phones. His fiancé was a lucky girl.

Connor was another story. Dread soured her stomach. He'd marched away under the assumption she'd sashay outside and wait like a pet dog. She could use the fresh air but to go outside would signal interest. If she could get Zoey and Sierra off the dance floor, they could act as buffers.

But how would she pull them away from the two luscious men they'd managed to latch onto? If they only knew who these guys were. On second thought, they could take care of themselves. Their werewolf dance partners should be the wary ones.

Despite Connor, she needed to escape the hot gym. She'd deal with him when the time came.

The outdoor patio where she and Ryan had lunch yesterday had transformed. Fairy lights in tree branches blended into the night sky and created a starry canopy. Candles flickered in jars on each table. A magical wonderland.

She chose the farthest seat from the gym door

and placed Ryan's jacket on the bench beside her. She traced her finger around the beautifully hand-sewn feathers.

Except for one or two wolves, she'd never seen anyone in their shifted form. She couldn't wrap her brain around what it would be like to see either brother as a falcon. It would never happen, so she might as well pitch the thought.

She ran her hand over the curls that took an hour to style, realizing humidity had flattened them against her head like plastic wrap on gelled salad. She wound her hair into an impromptu chignon and repositioned the flower.

As she fanned her neck hoping to capture the evening breeze, the seat next to her dipped under someone's weight.

Instinctively, she moved away. She'd had all the body contact she could stand with Connor.

"This is much better. Mind if I wait here a minute?" Ryan settled his legs under the table.

Her head whipped toward him. Under the twinkling lights, his muscular arms, covered with a hint of dark hair, sent ripples through her.

"No offense, but strutting on a stage was not fun. And I'm sorry about that paparazzi scene," he said.

"No offense taken."

He cracked a smile. "Seeing your face when I walked out on stage was the best part."

What did he mean? "Wonder where Connor is?" Though she was in no hurry to see him.

"He's suffering a FADS attack," he said.

"What's that?"

"Falcon attention deficit syndrome."

Jess's laugh exploded. "You made that up. But it fits."

Ryan's phone buzzed and he checked the message. "Doesn't look like my brother's making an appearance."

Had Connor's fiancé arrived and swept him away? Or, had he run off with another woman? Don't let it be Sierra or Zoey. For his sake, more than theirs.

"He's heading to the emergency clinic. He

slipped on spilled ice. Might have a broken wrist."

She'd hoped he'd disappear, but not something serious. "Should somebody go with him?"

Ryan kept reading his phone screen. Over the rising music volume, he nearly shouted, "Somebody's texting on his phone. He says to stay and enjoy the party. And that he owes you a drink—." The music stopped.

"And a dance." In the deafening silence, his words hung like icicles.

The band started a slow song, a pleasant change from the thumping stuff. The supers' sensitive ears must be rejoicing.

"If it wouldn't be a huge disappointment, I might be a half-way decent substitute for my brother," he said.

Substitute for what? "You mean, a dance?"

Ryan unwound from his seat and held out his hand. "I may not be as smooth as the Boston men you've dated, but I might surprise you."

His offer was surprising enough.

"I'm not sure we should do this," she said.

"Think my dancing is that bad?"

"Ryan, your brother told me you're engaged."

His hand dropped to his side. "She and I weren't right from the start. It didn't last six months. I don't know why he told you that."

Was this another game between the Ford brothers? Which version was the truth? If her heart had its way, she needed to believe Ryan.

She grasped his hand. His smile widened as he helped her stand. He nestled his hands on her lower back as she placed hers on his shoulders. When his cheek grazed her temple, current surged through her.

Giggling after a false start with her foot on his, they settled into a gentle, rhythmic sway. Graceful and effortless, he took the lead.

In his arms, the last days' anxiety dissipated. His strong arms tightened around her and more electricity skittered up her spine.

What was happening? Had his woodsy cologne become an irresistible aphrodisiac? She flicked her jade ring remembering she was in Nocturne Falls.

THE FALCON FINDS HIS MATE

For all she knew, this was a magical spell. But shifters don't cast spells.

"See the Bear Moon?" His whisper tickled her ear.

Full and bright, the sphere crested the pines. She tucked her head into his shoulder, filling her nose again with his musky scent. When his chin crossed her forehead, her body thrummed.

She should step away, but held in his comfortable embrace, she couldn't, or wouldn't, move. His warm breath crossed her wet lips and a craving chill ran over her.

In an instant, his mouth was on hers; his lips testing. His tongue skimmed the soft lining inside.

Her hands slid around his neck and pulled him tight. Their kiss deepened as their tongues danced. His fingers floated up her neck, and then laced in her hair, making small circles and ratcheting her longing.

Every reason to stop evaporated like raindrops on hot pavement. Rational excuses exploded. She wanted this.

And she didn't. How had she let this happen? The sultry night. His strong body against hers. Their mingling breath.

Wake up.

This is a shifter.

CHAPTER TEN

"What's gotten into you?"

Solange Ford's unmistakable shriek filled the air, breaking Jess and Ryan's embrace like a pin stick in a balloon.

"Your brother is in the emergency room, and you…you are dallying with this…human." Solange spat out the word as though she'd gulped coffee grounds.

Ryan stepped between his mother and Jess as Solange moved toward them, her head framed by her open hands. "You've taken this too far."

Jess backed into a trash can sending it rolling across the tennis court. She had no disease on the

CDC alert list. She bathed daily. She didn't belch in public. Was she that undesirable?

No secret what the woman meant. A non-shifter didn't meet Ford standards. Same old story. Prejudice still choked people like Solange. What a blessing to go away to college and live in a mostly human world.

Solange waved her hand in Jess's direction. "Miss Callahan, I suggest you go before anyone sees you."

"You're the one who should leave, Mother."

Jess's rage seethed. She'd been swayed by the moment; the moonlight; the nearness of this man. But she wouldn't take any crap from Solange Ford.

"I'll leave. But not because you *dispatched* me. I spent the last week working my tail off. I'm dead tired. And I don't need a dime's more of your family feud."

"Jess, wait," Ryan called.

Marching into the gym, she halted halfway to the exit. With a disgusted groan, she remembered Elvis brought them here. She'd have to call him for a ride home.

"Jess." Ryan had followed her.

Where were Sierra and Zoey? She had to get out of here before he sugar-coated Solange's conniption.

Jess flinched as he touched her arm. She cast furtive glances, hoping no one was watching them.

"She was way off base," he said.

If he thought she'd answer, he had a long wait. Her voice hitched, competing with trapped sobs she would not allow to escape. Shaking her head was all she could manage.

"I'll call you tomorrow. We'll straighten all this out," Ryan said, his voice glazed with regret.

Still unable to speak in coherent sentences, Jess waved him away. Any bud between them that tried to bloom had yielded to Solange's knife.

Ryan's words faded into the crowd as she made her way to the serving table where Zoey and Sierra were drinking syrupy fruit punch. A shame this party was alcohol-free. Jess could use a stiff drink.

"He's more adorable up close than on stage,"

Zoey said.

"Who?" Jess asked.

"Give me a break. Falcon guy," Zoey said.

"He looked like he could eat you like a candy bar." Sierra scanned Jess's hair. "Maybe he did."

Jess tucked a curl behind her ear, realizing half her hair had fallen out of the chignon. And the silly flower was gone; probably squashed under Solange's foot.

Should she give Ryan a chance to explain? She peeked over her shoulder, but he was gone.

"I knew him and his brother at Harmswood." Jess rewound her hair.

"No wonder that's all you talked about your whole freshman year," Zoey said.

They had the brothers mixed up but why bother telling them. Her gut was still taut after Solange's tirade. Though neither Ford meant anything to her, there was some satisfaction that both noticed her tonight. And had kissed her.

"Conner seems like a real player," Sierra said.

"I didn't think that at all," Zoey said. "He's hot

if you ask me."

Sierra sputtered her drink. "You're kidding. He eye-groped every woman in the place, even after he landed on the floor."

"Like you weren't sizing up men," Zoey said.

"Connor's the one I had the crush on," Jess said, though the other women didn't hear.

For the short moment, when she caught Connor's eye at Harmswood, there'd been rumblings that Solange planned to cause trouble.

Two innocent dates and Solange had browbeaten Connor so that a third never happened. Nothing had changed. Solange still had her talons in her sons.

For too long, Jess road a guilt pony. Not rich, cute, or smart enough. Crazy nonsense.

"So what about falcon guy?" Sierra primped her hair. "Is he yours?"

Protective jealousy pricked her. Why? Ryan was not 'hers'.

If Sierra, the cultured ambassador's daughter who grew up in Europe, and thought Boston was unsophisticated, wanted to chase after a falcon-shifter from North Georgia, then by all means.

Solange would be on that like a fly on a gooseberry pie. What fun to watch from a far distant galaxy.

"Knock yourself out," Jess said.

Sierra, the feminist pirate, slinked toward the courtyard; each step calculated like a cat after a robin. Except she was stalking the fastest predator bird on earth.

"Well, the girl still has the moves," Zoey said.

Jess spun the jade ring with a notion to slip it off and glimpse the scene ahead. She shouldn't let this happen to a friend. Ryan, on the other hand, deserved it.

"Let's grab some water. I have a feeling we'll be waiting," Zoey said.

Water at last. "Don't move a muscle."

In the front courtyard, Zoey sipped her water as she wiggled the gold dress down. "This wasn't the best costume. Next time, talk sense into me."

Jess was the least qualified to talk sense into

anyone after letting Ryan kiss her.

Sierra rejoined them, Ryan's tweed jacket slung over her shoulder like a souvenir. She grabbed Jess's water and took a long drink. Amen and amen.

"Take the rest," Jess said.

"You didn't stay long," Zoey said.

"Nothing out there but crickets." Sierra handed the jacket to Jess.

A lot had happened in seven years. Moving away. College. Dream job. Losing dream job. Breaking off two almost serious relationships. Moving home.

Being in Ryan Ford's arms.

Solange might be right.

What had gotten into her?

CHAPTER ELEVEN

Ryan's blood had reached boiling by the time he arrived home. His mother's Jag was parked in the drive; the hood still warm.

So, the holier-than-thou woman hadn't flown to Connor's bedside. His head pounded like a bass drum.

If he didn't get under control soon, he'd complete the change that started at Harmswood.

Aligned just below the surface, feathers threatened to penetrate his skin like sharp bayonets.

By sheer will, he reversed the emerging beak and talons. He would not give his mother the satisfaction of defeating him. He would not shift.

THE FALCON FINDS HIS MATE

It wasn't his fault that his mother played the lonely widow game to the hilt and took it out on her sons.

He, and Connor to some degree tried to cut her slack. But she's not the only one who missed their father.

He shook with resentment and contempt. Connor could slide in and out of falcon and felt nothing but a quick rush.

Ryan felt everything.

He had inherited his father's gene to change in slow, painful stages during anger shifts that took hours to reverse, and left him exhausted and lethargic for the next day.

This was no time to be incapacitated. But remembering how his mother had driven Jess away, control was impossible.

If he thought about something pleasant, he could reverse the shift.

He steered his attention to Jess Callahan. Beautiful, smart, and all woman. He'd been entranced. Her body snuggled against his. Her flowery perfume. How he had lost himself in her arms. Their comfortable, natural kiss.

What would it be like to have her in his bed? Her hair floating over her shoulders; one graceful arm draped over his chest. Their bodies coiled after making love.

Pain from the aborted shift finally subsided, leaving him aching to hold Jess again.

After mommy dearest's performance, Jess would be wise to run from any Ford that crossed her path.

His rage fading, he walked through the carved walnut front door and straight to the living room.

Bourbon-primed for another battle, Solange sat on a green velvet settee and tilted her crystal glass in his direction. "Join me?"

He waved off the drink and took a seat in his father's leather recliner.

"I can forgive this one dalliance, but I never want to see you cavorting like that with her ever again," she said.

"You make her sound like a cheap whore."

"I asked you to keep her away from Connor. I didn't mean for you to go to bed with her."

"What the hell are you talking about? It was a kiss." How could she talk about Jess like she was dirt? He had to be careful. Control the anger.

"And Melanie?"

Figures she would throw that in his face. Time to take his brother's advice.

"There's no more Melanie."

Her smug sneer peeled from her face. "What are you talking about? She's from a wonderful family."

"No engagement. No wedding." Lead chains unlocked their hold around his chest.

"After this blows over, I'm sure you'll see Melanie is the right woman who'll bear you fine offspring. Her family is well-connected."

Pity replaced his anger as the woman simpered.

"You should hear yourself. And nothing you can say will change things. It's over."

Fighting the shift left his head woozy, and his body drained. Had she tried to force his change to prove her point? Even Solange wouldn't stoop that low. Or would she?

He left her for the solitude of his workshop. He kept the lights off so moonlight could shine on the stallion.

If the Fareed invitation still held, he'd accept. Though it didn't match the winged freedom of soaring above the trees, a private jet ride to Dubai was tempting.

When, and if, he returned, he'd move the studio. He could go anywhere.

But he sure the hell wasn't staying in Nocturne Falls.

Echo brewed tea while Jess set out two cups. "You've been in this funk for three days. No wonder your friends went exploring on their own."

"I've been a fool," Jess said.

"Only if you take Solange seriously. Her nose has been in the air since I first met her."

Solange's words had stung for a while. It was

Ryan that Jess couldn't cut loose from her thoughts.

"How can Ryan or Connor stand living with her. One thing's certain, I realize how lucky I am to live with you, Nana. I'm not sure what I would have done."

"Precious, you're a strong woman who can stand on her own. It's been delightful to have you back."

The women drank their tea in peace, except for Crealde snoring at Echo's feet. Jess inspected the tea leaves that had settled in her cup.

She'd hedged for weeks on the tough conversation with her grandmother. Some reasons were legitimate. Repairs. Festival. Zoey and Sierra.

Most were not.

Her new job was around the corner. It could be in a week. Or a month. But Nana could no longer stay by herself. Upkeep. Maintenance. Running the shop.

"Let those worries go." Echo twirled the pearl cuff on the table.

Ice crystals formed in Jess's veins. "How long

has that been off?"

Echo set her eyeglasses next to the bracelet. If the wisdom in her eyes could be bottled, they'd be rich. "I've made arrangements."

Jess sprang from her chair. What arrangements? Was she hiding something? Was she sick?

"Oh, sit down. I'm fit as a fiddle, but not blind to the fact that I'm getting older, or that you're obsessed with my future. In due time this will all fall into place. You'll see. Now then, another cup?"

Echo's answer to any problem was tea. "You know the answer already."

In a convoluted way, Solange did her a service, though the woman's bluster about class and status was bogus, and all in Solange's head.

At the least, she owed Ryan, and herself, a chance to part as friends. In a weak moment, neither had used good judgment, though he was a damn good kisser. But it meant swallowing pride and taking the first step.

"Finish your tea and go talk to him. I'll

entertain Zoey and Sierra." Echo took the little wooden box from the drawer and shuffled the card deck.

"Nana, you aren't planning what I think?"

Echo angled her head and teased a grin.

CHAPTER TWELVE

Getting to the exclusive Wolf Creek shifters-only community was easy. Getting past the electronic gate? Not so much.

Jess pulled her car to a stop a few feet from the entrance and waited. She could, and probably should call Ryan to let her in. Even if she had his phone number, he wouldn't pick up if he saw her name on caller ID.

If she got through the gate, there was no guarantee he was even home. Misgivings rained over her. How stupid to stalk the guy like a high school groupie.

And how would she break the ice? 'Hey, there.

In the neighborhood and thought I'd drop by and say hello.' And when he threw her out on her butt?

If he wasn't home, she could say she tried to mend fences. Fences. Gates. Now or never.

When the first vehicle pulled up, she counted the seconds it took for the gate to activate, swing open and shut once the car passed. If she picked the right one, she might be able to draft through. The gate barely closed without hitting the slow pokes.

She needed to follow something small and fast. Something like the Harley she saw in the rearview mirror. If they were coming in here, that is. In case this was her break, she started the engine and put the car in gear.

The woman slowed the motorcycle to a stop at the Wolf Creek entrance and tapped a button on their bike. Shazamobam!

The gate glided open and the rider accelerated through the narrow space. Plenty room behind.

She seized the moment and gunned the gas. Incredible luck. But they should do something about that potential security flaw. Some other day.

Her GPS led her to the Ford address. Parked in front, she sat for a few minutes, rounding up courage. Like Crealde with a lizard, the chase was fun. What to do with the catch?

After pumping up her nerve, she walked to the arch over the driveway entrance. Perched on the end columns, cameras glared like twin cyclops.

She could imagine Solange sipping a drink, entertained by the security feed; her finger hovering over a switch that activated a larger-than-life bug zapper to destroy unwanted guests.

Passing through the gate, Jess flipped the bird to the cameras. Zap this.

Immaculate and manicured, the grounds were a vast difference from her grandmother's jumbled herb and flower garden. Where Echo's was eclectic and welcomed all, the Ford garden reeked of look-but-don't-touch. And it was eerily quiet. Not a sound anywhere except her own disembodied footsteps.

Jess halted where the driveway split. One way led to the front door. The other, to the garage where she'd heard Ryan had a workshop.

Covered in doubt, Jess couldn't take another step. What had she been thinking sneaking around like a thief? The brilliant shine on her peacemaking plan tarnished to a flat gray.

Appearing from nowhere, a half dozen butterflies spun and fluttered around her, circling so close she felt a breeze from their wings. To her delight, two landed on her hand for an instant, then took flight toward the street.

If she could believe the stories she'd heard as a child, butterflies meant angels were close. Good timing. Her stomach stood ready to launch.

So far, the angelic protection worked. No one had loosed lethal, spike-collared dogs. No armed, camouflaged soldiers jumped out from the hedge.

She scanned the house. No green-eyed monster peered from a second story window, though she sensed a foreboding vibe. Nonsense. How could a house have a vibe? Stress was anteing up its game.

She squared her shoulders and saluted the sky. "Thanks, team. If you have a few minutes, would it be a problem to hang around a little longer?"

From his window, Ryan watched in disbelief. How had Jess Callahan gotten this far into the estate?

In the sunlight, her hair shined like copper threads. Seeing her surrounded by butterflies nailed it. She was too pure for this dysfunctional family.

The skinny little wallflower had grown into an incredibly attractive woman. His mother was right. Jess had no business being associated with the Fords, but not for Solange's reasons.

So, what brought her here? He wiped his hands on a rag. Was she here for another go at his mother?

A sports car's whirring engine grew louder as it came down the driveway. His brother's timing never ceased to amaze.

Connor leaned against his Porsche, talking to Jess, probably milking his injury for all it was worth.

Keep going, Connor. Play the last sympathy

card. Jess had too much class to kiss and tell. On the other hand, seeing Connor's face when he found out about their kiss? Worth a million.

Holy bloody Sunday.

Connor had touched his lips to Jess's wrist.

Ryan's neck arteries bounded as he threw the shop towel on the floor. He stormed out the door, then slowed to a saunter. What's the rush?

The woman had the right to talk with any man she wished. Nothing bound them as a couple. Their moonlight kiss had been an impulse.

Ryan summoned his 'hello friend' voice. "Morning."

The three exchanged greetings, though Connor's eyes never strayed from Jess. Not a good omen.

"A little far from town, aren't you? I suppose you were just in the neighborhood?" Ryan asked.

Jess's eyes darted between the brothers. "Something like that."

"I invited her to tour Mother's home. Not every day you see a house decorated like a sixties' vampire movie set," Connor said.

"And I told him I'd pass," she said.

"Wise move. Would you like to see my studio?" He winced. What woman would buy that 'come up and see my paintings' line?

"I'm sure she'll love schlepping around in a wood pile," Connor scoffed.

"Don't start." Ryan's hair bristled.

"Bro, I just meant—"

"Whoa, guys." Jess moved out of the way. "Perhaps I should let you two fight it out?"

Once again, Connor had baited him. And like a fool, he'd bit the hook. Another Ford skirmish. There would be no full-scale battle today.

He watched Jess take the arms-across-her-chest stance he remembered from the gym. The glance she sliced between him and Connor underlined her impatience.

He cast his brother an iron warning.

"What did I do?" Connor asked.

No sense waiting for the apology that would never come from Connor's mouth.

THE FALCON FINDS HIS MATE

"I came here to see your shop, Ryan. I hear you're quite a wood crafter. You must have thought I was pretty stupid that day in the gym," Jess said.

Stupid? Never. But it was hard to believe that she came here to see where he worked.

Conner threw his key fob in the air and caught it.

"Umm. Anybody know why Mother's on a rampage? Nothing to do with that party, is it?"

"Why do you say that?" A noticeable squeak strangled Jess's voice.

Connor rolled his eyes in pretended amazement. "Come on. Every supernatural at the party heard her. Our mother is unaccustomed to obeying inside voice rules. It's all over town what happened. Too bad I missed the show."

Ryan had played the semi-hermit since the Showcase. Either Connor knew something, or he was bluffing.

"Knows *what* happened?" Jess's peaches and cream complexion went tomato red.

Connor raised his casted arm. "Hey, I was in

the ER, remember?"

Could Connor jack-hammer his last nerve any harder? "You have something to say, say it," Ryan said.

"Oh, my wounded arm. But if you insist. The story is you two found a cozy dance floor all to yourselves. And dear Mama caught you in a little lip lock. To have been a mouse under the table."

The sinews in Ryan's neck steeled. "I think it's time you left."

"Have fun, you two." Connor gave a sharp salute and went inside the main house.

Speechless like the concrete gargoyles downtown, Jess and Ryan stood silent.

Finally breaking the stillness, Jess said, "That was lovely."

Lovely wasn't the word on the tip of Ryan's tongue. Curses rolled in his head, none he could repeat aloud.

"Glad you can't read my mind," he said, hoping she didn't. Did her reassuring smile mean she can't, or she could? "After all that, you did make the trek out here. What *was* your plan?"

"Mostly, to apologize for running out on you," she said. Her cheeks had lightened from red to pink.

"My mother's the one who owes an apology. She wears prejudice like a badge."

"If that had happened seven years ago, I'd be hiding in a cave by the falls. I'm not a mousy little kid any longer. Solange proved that."

How could Jess be so generous. "You owe no apology."

"Perhaps. But I do want to see your studio."

Afternoon sunlight cast a spotlight on the magnificent wooden horse, polished to a marble shine. Every detail was seamless. Alive.

His voice tinged with sadness, Ryan explained it was commissioned and would ship next week.

"You don't want to let him go, do you?" She asked.

"Sometimes releasing something you love is the only option."

CHAPTER THIRTEEN

Spiders crawled up Jess's spine. Ryan didn't mean loving a stallion. Time to straighten things out before they stumbled into quicksand.

Fingers interlaced behind her, she edged to the front door with an eye to an escape route. "I need to talk to you about something else."

"No need." He fiddled with his tools. "The kiss shouldn't have happened."

Of all the things he could have said, that? Shouldn't have happened? "Why not?" She popped her palm over her mouth. Uh. Oh.

His hands froze over his workbench. "What did you say?"

THE FALCON FINDS HIS MATE

Her eyes darted around the room's four corners then froze on a door that was slightly ajar; a bedroom. Coming here may have been a huge mistake. But around him again, her anger dissipated and in its place, desire.

He coaxed her arms forward. "After further consideration, why not, indeed?"

With a gentle touch, he ran his hands up her arms and pulled her close. Then he glided his fingers along her jaws, softly tilting her head toward his. His lips grazed hers. Questioning. Wanting more.

Though her hands found their way around his neck, his hunger challenged her common sense. If she gave in, any caution messages from the universe would be forever silenced.

If…His lips sealed over hers.

She…Their tongues played.

Gave in…A guttural moan rose from his chest.

Jess broke the kiss. "Wait. We have to stop."

Eyes half shut, Ryan complied but didn't release her. "What's wrong?"

That was just it. Nothing was wrong. Jess had built a case for apologizing to Ryan. The plan was to say good-bye, not to be in his arms again.

Every automatic piston in her body had fired. Her breasts had swelled against his chest. A heaviness between her legs cried for relief. And his growing need responded.

"Jess."

His deep voice wrapped around her like a warm comforter. She rested her forehead against him as he rubbed small circles on her back.

After a long moment, he asked, "Is it because I'm a shifter?"

She wanted to shout 'no' to him; to the world; to herself. The truth was, she couldn't.

"Maybe," she whispered.

"What am I right now?"

"A man." Fully human, gorgeous, and handsome.

His hand ran down her thigh, paused, then lifted her leg to his hip. She raised the other leg, locking her feet around him.

THE FALCON FINDS HIS MATE

With a firm grip on her bottom, Ryan carried her to his apartment threshold where they interrupted their kiss, both panting as his eyes searched hers for indecision.

She pulled him close, sealed her lips on his, as he kicked open the door.

While Ryan took a business call, Jess waited outside on the small brick patio. She traced the filigreed pattern on a wrought iron table; every curve matched her twisting thoughts.

The plan had been to strike a peace deal so she wouldn't have to duck around corners every time she saw him.

Instead, she'd gone willingly to his bed and didn't regret a moment. She'd never forget this day. Nor would her lips, swollen from their kisses.

Or how her skin prickled where he had caressed her body, or how firm and full he felt inside her.

With the afterglow fading, she realized they

acted like crazed teenagers, and that she'd made love to a falcon shifter.

But the afternoon brought it home how she'd obsessed on the wrong brother. She wanted to laugh, but remembered the Ford estate wasn't a place where laughter seemed welcome.

Shadows lengthened and shaded the little patio. She checked the time and messages on her phone. Though they skipped lunch, their appetite had been more than satisfied.

Another car on the driveway caught her ear. It wasn't Connor's.

Solange slammed her car door. "I should have guessed that rattle trap parked on the street would belong to somebody like you."

"What the hell's your problem, Mother?"

Jess jumped at Ryan's booming voice behind her. 'What now?' she mouthed as Ryan slipped his arm around her.

"What is that woman doing here?" Solange sputtered.

"My guest."

"And why?" Solange asked.

Jess waited for his reply. This better be good.

"Special delivery from Carpe Diem," he said with a twinkle in his eye.

"What could they possibly have in that little shabbytique that we could use?"

Shabbytique? The Carpe Diem?

Solange didn't miss a beat. "What were you and that little wench up to?"

Jess's stomach twisted. Fists tight by her side, she stepped toward the old bat. Or falcon. Whatever she was, she had a Texas-sized bug up her behind, and Jess meant to shove it higher.

Ryan's grip on her arm saved her from assault and battery. "My guests are not your concern," he said.

Ignoring Jess as though she was an ivy-filled urn along the driveway, Solange barked, "This plan has gone completely wrong. I am so disappointed in you, Ryan."

Jess cut a glance at Ryan, who still gripped her arm.

"Mother, this is not the right time."

Solange's eyelids narrowed as she looked down her nose.

Jess wiggled from Ryan's grip. "Right time for what?" This was all too bizarre. "And in case you missed the news bulletin, Solange, the wench you're talking about is standing here."

"Fine. It will be much easier to hear this from me," Solange said.

Though the temperature still hovered in the nineties, Solange's dark stare sent a frigid blast through Jess. Ryan reached for Jess again, but she stepped away, uncertain who to trust.

Solange stood tall and jutted her chest. "Connor is getting married in a few weeks to a delightful girl. We didn't want him unnecessarily distracted. I asked Ryan to help keep you away from Connor, though he took it too far."

Ryan had done well on his assignment. "So I was a problem to be dealt with." Solange had used a sophisticated tactic and quite effective. Ryan had risen to the occasion and knocked Connor right off the radar. "I have to hand it to you both. What an elaborate scheme."

Jess was half-way down the driveway before Ryan caught up with her.

"I never agreed to her plan. If anything, I wanted to keep Connor from hurting you again," he said.

Jess kicked a pebble into the bushes. How dare this little rock try to escape from Solange's thorny rose bed?

Solange was a master at manipulation and wasn't above pitting her sons against each other. Maybe the apples didn't fall far from the tree.

He'd showered her with politeness, tenderness, and sincerity. Part of an act?

She snapped her gaze to Ryan. "Thanks for your sacrifice. Hope it wasn't too painful."

"Cut it out, Jess. What happened between us was, and still is, from my heart."

But after all, Ryan Ford was a shifter. For him, changing between stranger and lover might be as simple as turning from man to falcon.

"And I opened my heart to yours. For the last time."

CHAPTER FOURTEEN

Jess threw her car keys across the kitchen counter and watched as they slid over the edge and into Crealde's food dish.

Strung along by a mother and son collusion. Why didn't she see through this before now? Those Ford con artists didn't deserve her anger, but they were getting a dose anyway.

They weren't going to drag her down. Her smartest decision had been to move away from Nocturne Falls and people like Solange. The sooner she left again, the better.

"What on earth is wrong?" Echo asked.

Bile spun up her throat as she cleaned up

kibble. "I suspect you know."

Echo raised her arm to show her cuff bracelet. "I had clients all day. Would you like some tea and we can talk?"

Jess heaved a sigh, pulled a chair from the table, and displaced Crealde. With a disgusted growl, he thumped to the floor.

Everywhere she went today she stirred up disaster.

Neither spoke while lemon balm tea brewed in one of Echo's twenty-six teapots.

So many Nana talks at this table, long before Jess knew what her grandmother's gift was. Or her own.

"Precious, you seem a million miles away," Echo said.

If only she were.

"So, are you going to tell me what happened?" Echo asked.

Was the story worth telling? She'd already replayed it a thousand times since she left the Ford estate; every time the ending was the same. She took another sip of the aromatic tea. "How have you managed to survive in this town?"

"Whoa. Wait just a minute. We don't have pointy ears, or the ability to live in the water, or retractable fangs, or whatever. But our remarkable gifts rival anyone. Is it time to break out the party hats?"

Nana threw the first pity party one afternoon when Jess came home from school, teary eyed after a snubbing from one of the 'rich girls.'

They'd worn paper hats, drank root beer, and ate lemon ginger cookies all afternoon. By bedtime, she'd forgotten all about the spiteful school bullies.

"I'll be fine," Jess said.

"I'm about ready to take this bracelet off, so you better start talking."

Jess's heart pinched to see the woman's pixie face in mock anger. She refused to think about the day she wouldn't be farther away than a text message.

Without the cuff, Nana could read every thought, including lovemaking with Ryan Ford. Not ready for that.

"I can't tell if I'm enraged or outraged," Jess said.

Echo roiled a laugh. "All the same coin. Zoey and Sierra borrowed my truck and drove out to the Sanctuary but they'll be home any minute. My advice? Get your pretty selves dressed up and go out on the town."

How would skull-quaking music in an airless nightclub fix anything after a long afternoon in Ryan's arms? And a disgusting joust with Solange.

But what would they do here? Have a mani-pedi marathon and watch Nana's 'Charmed' CDs?

As she started to her bathroom for a hot bath, Jess remembered the cards and Zoey and Sierra. "Did they have a reading?"

Echo finished her tea and dabbed her lips with a napkin. "I can't violate client confidentiality."

And there was her answer.

Zoey adjusted her off-the-shoulder hot-pink

top. "Is this too much skin?"

Sierra layered eyeshadow. "Depends on your objective. No shoulder; no interest. One shoulder; maybe, maybe not."

Jess sat cross-legged on her bed. Not quite up for this, she had elected for simplicity; black leggings, flats and a silk blouse that floated over her halter top. A touch of lipstick and a splash of mascara. Maybe her friends could party after making love, but Jess was having second, third and sixteenth thoughts. But it might be time to take a lesson from them and get this behind her.

Sierra pointed her eyeshadow brush toward Zoey. "And remember what showing both means?"

Zoey pulled the blouse over her shoulders. "Forget that."

Jess warily straightened her blouse higher, too.

"Too bad Elvis can't take us," Sierra said as the three women crammed into Jess's tiny car. "His Cadillac was awesome."

"At the Sanctuary I heard somebody talking about Insomnia," Zoey said.

Jess had hoped they'd never bring that up. However, after Nana's pep talk, Jess appreciated that her supernatural ability was as good as anyone's. About time she asserted herself around this town before she left.

If anyone even thought about asking why they should be allowed inside, Jess could remove her ring and manifest a little picture in their honor. One or two visions and they'd be set.

No. She couldn't dishonor her grandmother by using the gift as a trick.

She'd let her Insomnia membership expire years ago. "If there's a line, we can always go somewhere else."

"Whoohoo. Barhopping like the old days," Sierra said.

If, and a big if, they got past the bouncer, what then? Members were not costumed theme park employees. These were breathing and living supers having fun in their own watering hole.

Water. She had to convince them to drink more water.

THE FALCON FINDS HIS MATE

On the industrial side of town, Jess found a parking spot a block from the building.

"Where are we?" Zoey hunkered down in her seat. "That sign says Caldwell Manufacturing."

"You wanted Insomnia. Well, we're here." Jess needed to clamp the attitude. It wasn't her friends' fault she'd hopped into bed with a falcon.

Zoey and Sierra huddled behind her as Jess tapped the code, grateful she still remembered it and that it hadn't changed. They went through the first door, past unmanned equipment, to a freight elevator.

"This can't be right. Shouldn't we hear some music or something?" Sierra cautiously peered around. "Are you pranking us?"

Jess pressed the elevator button, the door opened, and she stepped inside, alone.

"What's the problem? Scared?"

"Nope," Sierra and Zoey said in unison.

Jess was nervous enough for all three. "Then

get in."

In the basement, the elevator door opened to the lobby and just beyond, dance music, and wall-to-wall supers. And no crowd and no line.

Zoey and Sierra, smiles wide as the Mississippi River, were about to get their wish. And Jess was about to be sick.

CHAPTER FIFTEEN

One giant obstacle; the bouncer was a man Jess didn't recognize. The size of a double-door refrigerator, he sat on a stool, meaty arms crossed. Likely he was one of the town's gargoyles hired to enforce the club rules.

"Ladies, your ID." The man's voice boomed over the music.

Each produced a card. "These are all out of state. Who's the club member with you?"

Jess wiggled her finger for him to bend closer. "I'm staying with my grandmother. We own the Carpe Diem. I grew up here and went to the Academy. These are friends from college. I promised to show them our nightlife."

Her explanation didn't register. "I'm not sure this is the right place for you," he said.

Like she didn't know who came here. If she pushed and outed herself, no telling what her friends would do.

Sierra strutted toward him. "Let me handle this."

Jess grabbed her arm. "Uh, no. There are other places." Embarrassment bathed her. This guy was no match, even for Sierra.

"Is there a problem, Nick? These beautiful women are with me."

Someone held Jess's elbow. She whipped her head toward the source putting her nose-to-nose with Connor Ford's killer smile.

He leaned close to Jess. "Never thought I'd see you here."

Never thought she'd *be* here.

Sierra hooked her arm around Connor's and saluted the bouncer as they passed him.

Inside, Jess took three water bottles from a bin

by the door. "Remember our old rule? First drink of the night, water."

Connor led them to the VIP section then ordered drinks from the server.

"Amazing. You snagged Connor just like that. Well done," Sierra whispered in Jess's ear.

Right. Well done. She'd vowed never to have another thing to do with a Ford. And what happens? She 'snags' one. Staying home and painting her toenails had never appealed more than right now.

After a few minutes, the server returned with a bottle of white wine and filled their glasses.

Connor raised a toast. "Ladies, may the moon never catch you crying."

"This place is unreal," Zoey said as she sipped her wine. "People look like they jumped right out of a fantasy movie."

Real, unreal and fantasy were just differing perspectives in the Insomnia.

"Get out and dance," Connor said. "In this crowd, nobody cares if you have a partner or not."

"Come on," Zoey said as she tugged on her

friends.

"Thanks, but I'll sit this one out," Jess said.

As the girls disappeared onto the dance floor, Connor scooted close. "So, you recovered?"

Ice flash. From what? Making love to his brother? She eased away from him.

"I heard the whole thing in the driveway," Connor said. "Quite a scheme to keep us apart."

"She had a willing accomplice."

"Mother has a thing about mixing humans and shifters."

"She has a point. It wouldn't work."

"That's where you're wrong. And did I mention you look beautiful? How about the dance I owe you? If I'm right, our last one was in the Harmswood gym. That would be how many years ago?"

Well, that would be after college and three years in a job. They were in high school. "Somewhere around nine years and six months." But who's counting?

Connor stood, made a bow and offered his

hand. "May I?"

"I don't do bump and grind."

"We'll take it slow." He pulled Jess toward him.

"To club music?" Though it was low volume to accommodate the supers' sensitivity to anything loud, it was still high energy. Tonight, Jess was a low energy girl.

Overpowering, the scents of his cologne mixed with expensive leather car interior competed for oxygen. As his hands slid around her waist, she wondered what to do with hers. Place them on his shoulders? His back? Or let them dangle like noodles at her side?

If this was Ryan, she'd have known exactly where she wanted to hold him. But Connor?

Though he schmoozed her into this, it brought everything full circle. All these years wondering what it would have been like to be in his arms.

And now she knew. It left her flat.

Irish stout was meant to be sipped and savored, not chugged the way Ryan consumed it tonight.

On his second pint, he watched the foamy surge that was taking too much time to settle. Too much time for regrets.

After today, would he ever have a chance with the feisty woman who drove him over the brink? Unlikely. He ran his fingers down the pint glass, remembering how smooth Jess's skin had been under his touch. How she'd responded and given herself to him.

The one positive thing from this debacle, the private jet to Dubai sounded better and better.

"Don't look now, but Connor just blew in," the bartender said. "And you won't believe this. He took three women with him to the VIP section."

Connor's favorite spot. But three women? Ryan bet none was his brother's fiancé.

As the DJ switched to full-blown trance dance, the crowd went into a frenzy. Great for Connor, but hellacious for Ryan who preferred peace and quiet.

His head throbbed as he watched the dancers

gyrate like ghosts under the club's subdued light.

Among the arm-waving fanatics, Connor was slow-dancing. His old trick to throw women off their game. This man could never settle down with one woman. What was their mother thinking?

He paid his bar tab and wormed his way toward the door. One final look toward the dance floor convinced him he'd outgrown this lifestyle. Chalk up another lesson learned.

Have a nice time, Connor and whomever you're dancing with tonight.

Through an opening between the revelers, he saw Connor spin and dip his partner.

As people jostled around Ryan, the bouncer asked, "Ford, you coming or going?"

At this moment, he had no answer.

The 'whomever' dancing with his brother was the red-haired Jess Callahan.

Connor Ford had been her life's crush. But all Jess could think about was Ryan. His kiss. His strong arms holding her during their tender lovemaking. She wanted to believe that was real and not some charade to help his mother with her ridiculous 'plan.'

The music switched to something even more obnoxious.

"Mind if we sit down?" Jess asked.

At their table, Connor raised the wine bottle. "There's a little left."

"No, thanks." The first glass wasn't playing nice with her stomach after Connor's dramatic spin.

"Would you do me a favor?" She asked.

"Anything."

"I don't feel well." Zoey and Sierra were winding their way to the table.

"Can you drive my friends home? I don't want their night to end because of me. They leave the day after tomorrow."

A sly smile crossed Connor's lips. "No problem. You okay to drive home?"

"Yes, but Conner, these women are regular humans. Remember that."

"I got this," he said.

Amid veiled protests, Zoey and Sierra agreed to stay.

Once home, Jess changed into her sleep shirt, wiped away make-up and any trace of the Fords.

One last look at her phone. A message from the headhunter.

She read it twice.

A job. A real job.

In Boston.

She could finally leave Nocturne Falls.

That was a good thing. Yes?

CHAPTER SIXTEEN

No better way to combat stress than salted caramel ice cream. Jess had slurped through half the pint. Self-control told her to save some for later. But why? Would she gain ten pounds from the last three bites?

Why make excuses? Not the most nutritious dinner, but good. It had been a long day.

After breakfast, Zoey and Sierra and Jess had hugged, cried, and vowed to meet again before another three years passed. She missed them more than she'd imagined. The week had gone by too fast. And the house seemed so empty and quiet.

She'd spent the last hour in a phone interview

then had booked a flight to Boston for her on-site interview. If all went well, her first day was in three weeks, and a thousand miles away from Nocturne Falls.

She'd almost started fantasizing a life here, and for a few minutes, a life with Ryan Ford. Middle school daydreams. A clear sign it was time to move on.

A hundred minutiae. She'd have to find a new apartment somewhere on the Boston outskirts. She didn't relish two hours a day on a train, but she couldn't afford downtown, even though the new salary was twice what she'd made before.

But this meant leaving her grandmother. She could move to Boston and be with her. But Echo Stargazer anywhere else than in Nocturne Falls?

And where *was* her grandmother? She didn't mention any appointments or errands this morning after Zoey and Sierra left. It wasn't like her to be out this late in the afternoon.

"Jess, can you come down here? Closing time and we aren't supposed to cash out the registers." A store clerk's voice drifted up the staircase.

She tossed the empty ice cream carton into the recycle bin. "Be right down."

Jess flipped the Carpe Diem closed sign and locked the front door. Concern building, she scanned her text messages. Nothing. Another call to her grandmother's cell went to voicemail.

Still daylight for a few hours. Maybe she'd gone into the woods for a personal meditation retreat.

Even with Jess's lectures about traipsing out by herself, which Echo tended to ignore, it wasn't like her to disappear and not tell someone.

She paced the apartment from one end to the other, ending in the kitchen. Crealde knocked his food dish into the cabinet.

"Damn it. Don't spook me like that."

A soulful meow accompanied his brush at Jess's ankles. "I'm sorry, buddy. You're worried, too. And it's your dinner time. Where is she, cat?"

She didn't expect an answer, even in this town.

She fed Crealde then spread wrinkles from the

tablecloth where everyday people would sit slack-jawed while those little pictures appeared on Echo's cards.

A sudden hint of patchouli wafted around her. Where was that coming from? Nothing was left burning downstairs.

Something lingered from another time; though it seemed fresh.

If her grandmother didn't call or come home in the next few minutes, Jess would have to call the sheriff. What would she tell him?

She hadn't seen her grandmother since breakfast.

No phone messages.

Yes. She'd called Echo's friends.

No. Echo didn't keep a calendar.

Wandering through their rooms for the tenth time, Jess halted at her grandmother's bedroom door.

As big as life, smoke rose from three incense sticks standing upright in a glass jar on Echo's dresser.

She'd looked in this room not ten minutes ago.

How had Echo managed to sneak in and light those? She must have come up the outdoor stairs. If her grandmother was safe, who cared?

"You had me worried to death," she called. "Where were you?"

No answer.

The room was empty.

The curtains were drawn.

Then who lit the incense?

She forced herself to enter. Something sat in the middle of the bed.

Just like that card reading.

Cold sweat poured over her.

Crealde pushed past and jumped on the bed. He tapped his nose around the mysterious object; his soft meow confirmed it was safe.

She sat on the bed and switched on a lamp.

The cat's paw rested on a small leather book.

Inside was an envelope addressed to Jess, written in her grandmother's handwriting. She sat it unopened beside her.

THE FALCON FINDS HIS MATE

The book's fragile pages were reluctant to turn even with a tender touch.

The first entry was dated seventeen years ago; the day Jess's parents died.

Only four words: 'Today my heart fractured.'

She flipped the book shut and pushed it away. She never knew her grandmother kept journals.

And why was this left out in a conspicuous place?

Had her grandmother been interrupted while she wrote in it? Crealde hunkered into a ball next to her, resting a paw on the journal.

Those last ice cream bites ventured up Jess's throat. Both the envelope and the book were for her.

This was a lucid dream and all she had to do was open her eyes. But she was awake.

"Well, Crealde, I guess we read the letter."

Precious,

Master Cheng invited me to take a journey with him. I'm safe. And there's nothing to worry about, even though I know you will. I couldn't tell you before because you'd try to talk me out of this.

Always use your gift wisely. Give your love freely. Remember what I said about making people happy. Keep your heart open and trust your wisdom. I'll always love you and always be near.

Nana

PS. The house, Crealde, and Carpe Diem are all yours. Lock, stock, and cauldron. And, the cards are in the drawer.

Every untoward scenario scattered across Jess's mind. Had Master Cheng tricked her grandmother into running away with him? Was he a swindler? Had he taken her money? Was she being held against her will and made to write this note?

Had her grandmother pulled a classy hoax?

Or were these the arrangements she talked about?

"I don't get this."

Maybe the journal held more answers. With trembling hands, she reread the first entry, written the day her parents died. The next one a year later. Each of the seventeen entries was on the anniversary date.

THE FALCON FINDS HIS MATE

Her heart skipped. The next anniversary was in two weeks.

She petted the white cat sleeping beside her. This was no dream. It had all happened. Her grandmother was gone. Where? For how long?

What would she do without her? Nana was the only family she knew besides the uncle that refused to take her into his home all those years ago.

An avalanche of horribles coated her like sticky molasses. This huge house. The business. How could she manage this and still live in Boston? She couldn't just lock the door and walk away from Carpe Diem.

Remembering a half-bottle of Syrah in the kitchen, she poured a glass. After the second sip, she was ready to open the journal.

As hard as it had been to lose her parents, what grief her grandmother must have borne.

Though she visited this place every summer, Jess would never forget walking through the door days after her parents died. And her Nana's words, 'Welcome home.'

After a year, she stopped her nightly perch on her bedroom windowsill, watching for her father's blue car to pull in and take her to her real home.

With time and a grandmother's love, living in a magical world became her new normal.

This journal must have been Nana's way to cope. On each anniversary, there was a letter written to Jess's mother.

In them, Echo had told her daughter all the things Jess had done in the last year. Her accomplishments in school. Her sad and happy times. Her birthday parties. Harmswood Academy Awards. College scholarships. The first job.

All in the voice of a caring and proud grandmother.

Two hours later, and after crying sufficient tears to create a waterfall, Jess read the last lines, dated today.

'Your beautiful daughter is a smart, savvy woman who looks more like you every day. The store and dear Crealde are in the best hands I could ever imagine. Now I'm off.'

THE FALCON FINDS HIS MATE

Off to where?

CHAPTER SEVENTEEN

On schedule, the transport truck rolled to a stop in front of Ryan's door. He waved to the two men in the front seat; the driver and a member of the Fareed family.

After they had confirmed the packing instructions and flight schedule, Ryan gave the wooden statue one last polishing wipe.

With neurosurgeon precision, the men wrapped the horse in a protective blanket and bubble wrap, then laid it on a sisal bed. They sealed the crate and loaded it into the truck.

"Our plane departs at three," one man said. "It will be our family's honor for you to install this beauty in its new home."

Ryan leaned against the doorframe as he watched the van drive away. He worked on that stallion for months; bared his soul to this creature. Imbued it with his deep secrets. He couldn't let it make this trip alone.

Though Dubai was the world away, it would be a clean break to reset his life. When he had explained the plan to his mother, she had thrown a fit the size of Lake Erie.

Connor had asked if there was an extra seat.

There wasn't any reason to stay. He had money and could start over anywhere.

As he went through tool drawers, he decided everything could go in storage. Pandora Van Zant, the best real estate agent in town, could help coordinate this.

His passport and a few clothes in a suitcase and he'd be ready.

Except for one loose end.

He should call Jess Callahan and clear the air, though what good would that do?

What possessed him to think that she could live in the Ford world? Or want to speak to him again?

Why couldn't he shake how his lips fit on hers? How her soft velvety skin felt against him as they made love. How at ease they'd been in each other's arms afterward for an all-too-short time.

And how she looked dancing in Connor's arms.

Hell, his mother had done them all a favor. Better it ended before they made a foolish commitment.

Connor pulled up a stool and sat in the empty spot where the stallion had been. "Now that the object of your desire is gone, what's next?"

Ryan's heart jumped into his throat, then settled. Connor meant the horse.

"He's been my life for over a year, counting planning and sketching."

"Like I said, it's your best work. You decide to go with them?"

"I did, and I have a lot to do before the flight."

"I can help out here. It's not like I have a full schedule."

THE FALCON FINDS HIS MATE

With thousands invested in this workshop, how would his brother have the first clue what to do? "Just let Pandora handle it."

Connor opened a cabinet and held up the gaudy T-shirt. "You kept this? She never mentioned it again, did she?"

"We were spared."

That hideous shirt brought memories. Jess managing misfit stage hands and convincing him that misshapen wood chunks could become a forest.

And that a loner falcon might one day find a mate.

"Connor, there is one thing you might do for me."

"Name it."

"Take care of Jess."

"You're asking *me* to take care of her? Oh, this is where I came in. Mother's messed us both up."

"I saw you dancing with her at Insomnia. Looks like she finally got the man she wanted all along."

Connor screwed his face into a question mark.

"Who? Me? We had a dance. She used the old brush-off line. 'I don't feel well.' I helped her out and stayed with her two girlfriends. Man, those foxes can party. I was dragging butt to keep up."

"She went home? So, you two didn't…"

"Didn't what? You think there's something between her and me? Hilarious. It's not me she has the hots for."

Ryan beaded his eyes on Connor. Was there someone else in town she'd been seeing? "Then who?"

"Are you that clueless? She loves you, bonehead. And when will you realize you're in love with her?"

"Me? In love?"

"Hearts and flowers. Candy and perfume. All that jazz."

Wrong, bro. All wrong. "We've never even gone out on a real date," Ryan said. They'd skipped that step, unless sharing a food truck lunch counted.

"Unless you can shift into a trans-Atlantic falcon, in my opinion, you have a real problem on your hands."

He considered this a moment. No. He didn't have a problem. The world might. His mother might. But he didn't.

He spun the bench vice handle till it was tight. "Connor, you have plans for later? Say around three o'clock?"

CHAPTER EIGHTEEN

Reliable as London's Big Ben, and nearly as loud, Crealde's breakfast alarm caterwauled through the house.

The meow monster muscled between her legs as she poured chow into his dish. "All right, already."

If this cat, the center of his personal universe, missed Nana, it didn't show.

With Crealde crunching food in the background, Jess looked at her messages again. Two from the headhunter. A text from Sierra.

Nothing from her grandmother.

And nothing from Ryan.

What did she expect? She made it clear to him and his mother that she was done with that hot mess.

The world was bigger than Nocturne Falls. Time to blow this popsicle stand.

Wherever her grandmother was, she'd understand. It might be smart to keep Carpe Diem open for a while. She could hire a manager and still live in Boston.

Her phone buzzed. Her headhunter.

"Jess, where've you been?"

Right here in River City. Tending to business. Dabbling in a little magic. Accepting that her clairsentient grandmother had followed her Tai Chi master to another world. Trying to forget a certain shape-shifting falcon.

"It's been a little crazy here," she said.

"I have the perfect job for you. Why didn't I think about this before?"

Perfect intrigued her, but she'd already arranged a second interview in Boston. "Might be a little late."

"Oh, don't worry. That was just a phone interview. You can always turn it down. I can fix all that. A woman with your talent and keen insight make you a fit."

She'd made the emotional move to Boston and mentally gone real estate hunting. Everything was planned, almost to what she'd wear on the first day.

"This better be good," Jess said.

"It is. I promise. How about working with me? My business has grown so much that I can't handle it without help."

"Headhunter? Me?"

"We prefer to call it talent management."

Call it whatever she wants, it's still head hunting. Corporate matchmaking.

"I don't have a clue about this business," Jess said.

"We've all started somewhere."

There would be a salary and commission. Office expenses. And she could relocate to Boston whenever she was ready, or stay in Georgia and work from home. Say the word and the job was hers.

After the call, Jess showered and dressed. She had good reasons to leave Nocturne Falls. And good reasons to stay.

Head spinning, she tackled first things first; open the shop.

After the Carpe Diem staff arrived, Jess started her errand run. The DIY Depot for supplies to repair the upstairs toilets, and window caulk. Then the bank.

It had been an enormous job keeping up the house. Working with her hands all summer gave her a break from the trapeze swinging monkey troupe in her head.

But what about her grandmother? What if she didn't return? How could she leave Nocturne Falls without knowing where her grandmother was?

Luck would have it; she found a parking place within walking distance to the bank. The worry band around her chest constricted as she sat across from the vice president.

As the letter promised, the property and

inventory was hers; lock, stock, and cauldron. Every detail covered.

But the contract had to be signed no later than thirty days from the day Echo wrote the letter. "And if I don't sign, then what happens?"

The bank official placed his glasses on the table.

"Everything remains in her name and under her control until you take ownership. But if she's on an extended vacation, as you've said, and you haven't signed on, or before the deadline, and haven't taken ownership for any reason, this would go into court. It's possible that this would be considered property abandonment."

A powerful swimmer, Jess was way over her head in whitewater. Not yet noon and she'd been recruited by a recruiter to be a recruiter, misplaced her grandmother, and Carpe Diem was at risk.

On the upside, she found a two-for-one sale on toilet guts.

The Hallowed Bean was a short walk, and a double-espresso Monster Mocha iced latte called her name. This time she'd finish her darn drink without interruptions from any Fords.

Though the Bean wasn't the best place to sort through the half-pound portfolio, it had to do.

A frantic search on her phone for 'property abandonment' listed sites ranging from the ridiculous—a fool's guide to abandoning a home—to esoteric legalese mumbo-jumbo.

Why hadn't she asked more questions at the bank? Shock and denial perhaps?

Time to fast forward through the commercials.

There was a way through this, but she wouldn't resort to it for love or money. She could take off the ring and look for the story's ending. No. She'd figure this out like a regular human. One step at a time.

First, get home before closing. Besides, those toilet flappers wouldn't replace themselves.

As she bundled her papers and recapped her drink, Jess spotted Pandora Van Zant seated at a small table, toe-to-toe with Ryan.

Thought this was the day the horse shipped.

Was it gone already? Wasn't he going with it? And what's he doing with her?

Slow down, monkeys. Pandora's a newlywed, remember? No threat. No hanky panky. And, why was she concerned about Ryan's companions?

Compared to the drop-dead gorgeous Pandora, Jess, without a stick of makeup, in old work jeans and worn canvas shoes, looked like a rag bag. She spread her fingers and looked at her ratty nails. She needed a visit to Hair Scare for a manicure in a desperate way.

Manicured nails on the hands that would soon be dipping into a toilet tank? That made no sense. She curled her fingers into her palms.

He can't see her like this.

As she pressed the door open, she sensed someone behind her.

"I'll get that." A man's deep voice over her shoulder.

Standing on the sidewalk away from the tourist crowd, Ryan gently gripped her arm. "I tried to get your attention inside." His eyes dropped to the folder under her arm.

"I saw you. With Pandora," she countered, a bit sharp. Argh. She hadn't meant it to come out like that.

"It was business." His quizzical look confused her as he held her arm. "You have a minute?"

The clock in the town square struck the half-hour. "Not now."

He pulled his hand away, leaving her skin tingling from his touch. "I have to talk to you."

A collision with a pint-sized space trooper careened Jess into Ryan.

What undiscovered physics principle said that for every inch closer to this man's embrace, her desire for him exponentially skyrocketed? And this was no place for an erotic meltdown.

"Can it wait till morning? My place for breakfast?" Jess asked.

Shuffling the bank folder from one arm to the other, she wondered who channeled that invitation. Nana?

Jess wasn't ready to tell anyone that Echo

Stargazer had flown the coop. The hurt was still too fresh. Eventually, she'd find a reasonable way to explain it. Not in the middle of the street.

"Tomorrow morning it is. I'll bring something from Delaney's. See you around eight." With a riveting smile, he waved over his shoulder.

While he was picking up savories from the bakery, he could bring a gallon of understanding. Her news would top anything he had.

CHAPTER NINETEEN

Jess swung hangers across her closet rod looking for something that didn't make her look like a home-repair TV host.

Something nice; not too nice. This wasn't a fancy-schmancy affair. But she had invited Ryan to her house and it qualified as a real date.

Even with the high probability of it all melting away, she applied mascara, eyeliner, and coral lip gloss. Who was the giddy woman staring at her in the mirror? The same woman who'd stormed off the estate? But something kept tickling her heart that Ryan told her the truth. Nana perhaps? She could hope.

In the back of her closet was Ryan's jacket. She held the sleeve to her nose. It still held the scent of his cologne. What was that 'something important' he had to tell her?

Maybe she should wear the boho-girl dress that she wore the first time Ryan kissed her. A one-time-only outfit and besides, too costumey.

She grew up in Nocturne Falls, but dressing up like Halloween gave her heartburn.

Her meager selection didn't include frilly day-wear. White capris and a sleeveless teal top would work fine.

Anyway, the man had seen her in grubby work clothes and absolutely no clothes.

Ryan was due any minute and the whole reason for playing dress-up. She dashed to the kitchen where Crealde perched in the sink, running a paw across the window.

She should be furious with the huge fur-ball-with-legs shedding everywhere, but watching him make little cat barks and swipe across the glass at a squirrel on a limb was too funny.

"Out for you, bud." She lifted him to her shoulder and nuzzled his furry face. "Careful what you chase after; you might just get it. Then what?"

The screen door latch wiggled in her hand. "Come on. Is there nothing left around here that works?"

Add that to the list of whatever else planned to disintegrate today. Ryan and Crealde passed one another on the stairs.

"Morning," he said through the screen. "That's quite a big cat."

A pop followed by his stunned look at the broken door latch in his hand squeezed a laugh from Jess.

"Welcome to the crumbling house of horrors," she said.

He placed a bakery box on the kitchen table set with Nana's everyday dishes.

"I can fix that door," he said.

She shrugged and gestured to a seat. "I'll deal with it later." This place had to get spiffed up to sell, but her time and energy were about gone.

As she scanned the croissants, sweet buns and fruit tarts, her mouth watered. And perhaps a little bit for the man across from her.

Their fingers met on the same pastry.

"Sorry," he said.

"You first." Such a nice homey exchange. No one would guess they'd made love or, that she told him she never wanted to see him again.

As Nana would say, 'details, details.'

But, politeness was about to take a nosedive. He just snatched the only Ravishing Raspberry tart in the box.

In a gallant gesture, Ryan cut it and placed half on her plate. "I owe you. Remember the day I took all your onions?"

She was losing ground on her resolve not to fall for a man who had just shared heaven. After taking a bite, jam dribbled down her chin.

He handed her a napkin. "Good, aren't they?"

Discretion tossed to the wind. Jess devoured her half tart, a whole croissant, which she slathered in butter, an apricot filled bun and a second coffee.

Ryan barely touched his.

She didn't care what he thought about her ravenous appetite. The splurge was justified. She'd be on her feet in the shop and home repair mode after closing. And probably pull an all-nighter reviewing legal documents.

Besides, gooey sweets helped distract her from a missing grandmother and the man sitting across the table. Apart from that, the pastries were damn delicious. And so was he.

"So where's Echo this morning?"

His question knotted her overfull stomach.

"Running errands," she lied.

"I bet she's not looking forward to you leaving."

Her Nana's disappearing act was an odd way to show it. "More coffee?"

Ryan covered his cup. "Will you take a walk with me?"

He hit that one far outfield. "If you like." Though his reason escaped her.

The drought in full sway, the county was still

hot as Hades. But not in Echo's garden.

Jess glided her hands over the bushes growing along the flagstone path. Would new owners appreciate these grounds as much as her grandmother does? Or, past tense. Had.

"The further we walk, the further we seem to be from town," he said. "We're in the middle of a forest, and we only walked a few yards from the house."

"She planned it that way." With help from the fairies.

The path wound through a thicket until it ended where stones surrounded a fire pit.

Cobalt blue bottles hung throughout the trees and showered midmorning sun around them.

Jess's heart tugged. This was her grandmother's sacred circle.

Sometimes Echo spent the night in this place communing with her guides. Was this the spot where she'd been convinced to walk into the ether?

Ryan took a seat on a wooden bench, his hands clasped between his knees. "I need to explain."

THE FALCON FINDS HIS MATE

She sat across from him. "I don't want to go through this again."

"Can't blame you. My mother can be pretty snarky."

Snarky. What a creative word. "She certainly has a strong will."

Ryan stifled a laugh. His eyes searched hers, leaving unfinished sentences.

She spun the ring around her finger vowing not to surrender.

"It was her idea to keep you and Connor apart, but I wouldn't have any part of it. You have to believe me."

Jess found a stick and dug around in the pit. Nothing had burned in here for weeks. She did believe him. But this wasn't the barrier.

"She's short on diplomacy, but she had a point. You and I—"

"Let me finish what I came here to say." He moved to kneel beside her. "I'm not good at small talk. You think there's a future for us?"

On his knees asking about their future? A

sudden whirlwind tossed the leaves around them as his question spun in her mind. What could she say that wouldn't hurt him? That was the last thing she wanted.

"Ryan. What about your mother? She's wedged like a boulder between us. You really think that would change?"

Ryan's face clouded. "I can handle her." The sadness in his voice undermined his promise.

No matter how hard she tried to weed them from her thoughts, Solange's words had taken root.

"A falcon and a human. What kind of life would that be?"

"I'm not like Connor who changes as the mood strikes. And I can't imagine a life without you."

How could she tell this man, who should carry a weapons' license for those deadly dark eyes and long eyelashes, that the point wasn't who shifted or why? It was the whole bizarre idea of people changing into animals that freaked her out.

He cupped his trembling hands around hers.

"What I'm trying to say, Jess, is that I'm in

love with you."

CHAPTER TWENTY

Jess gasped for air, hoping it would resuscitate her. Ryan's rock-steady gaze and grip around her hands blew any chance to evade the question.

The man sure the hell wasn't good with small-talk.

A branch above them cracked and fell to the ground, barely missing them as it landed in the fire pit. Shaking, Jess bolted up and tossed the broken limb into the brush.

Ryan laid his hand on her arm. "Okay?"

"Just a little rattled." Less about the dead branch; more about how what he'd told her changed everything.

She scanned overhead. "Guess I need to hire a tree man, too."

"This wasn't exactly how I'd planned this." He picked a twig from her hair.

She put her arms around him and rested her cheek against his chest. His heart raced alongside hers, at breakneck speed.

Did he honestly think that they could be compatible? So endearing. So naïve.

She loosened her hold. The absolute truth, loving him terrified her.

"Ryan."

He closed his eyes and bowed his head. "I understand."

"It's not what you think." Though it was. "Things aren't going so well in my world."

Jess jammed her hands into her pockets. Time to tell someone that Nana's skipped town. Crossed the ridge to the next village. Eloped with a leprechaun. All more plausible than the truth.

She took a long breath. "Nana's not running errands." At least not in this world.

She could melt at the caring look in his eyes. Gentle. Kind. And full-throated sexy.

"Then where is she?" He asked.

"I don't know."

"What do you mean you don't know?"

She wished for a sane answer. "I came home two days ago and she was gone. Not a trace." Aside from a letter and a journal.

"Is she staying with someone?"

"No."

"Her pickup's in the driveway. She couldn't have gone far. Did you call the sheriff? Two days is a long time at her age."

The urgency in his questions reignited her panic. Time to explain or he'd have Sheriff Merrow here in a Nocturne Falls minute.

"You need to sit down. This might be hard to believe," she said.

"This is Nocturne Falls. Try me."

Jess tucked a handful of hair behind her ear and swallowed. "Nana is clairsentient."

"Not news."

"And she has spirit guides."

"So does half the town."

"I think she's crossed to another dimension with her Tai Chi teacher."

He squinted. "Well, that's a little different."

She brushed a stray leaf from her shoulder. "Nana transferred the Carpe Diem to me."

His right eyebrow raised. "That's serious. What's this do to your plans?"

Foul them up. "I can't think straight." About this or love.

"Jess, have you tried looking for her with your gift?"

Sweat bloomed over her. How could she admit that she hadn't? He'd think she was a fool, or worse. She cast her gaze to the ground and shook her head.

She'd spent her adult life trying to be a regular human, and all summer keeping an arm's distance from everyone in Nocturne Falls. Humans work through problems using their own wits, not magic.

Right. Sure. Who was she kidding?

She was petrified to call up images. When she was young, random visions were so real that they'd made her ill. Before discovering the ring's blocking effect, she'd thought she would go crazy.

"I'm afraid to try. I don't know what I'll see," she said.

"If I stay with you, would that make it easier?"

The only way to find out was to try. "Promise you'll be here even if something weird comes through? I haven't done this in a long time."

He stood behind her and placed his hands on her shoulders. "I'm not going anywhere."

She slipped the ring from her finger and waited. And waited. Not a single picture came through.

Hello, out there. It's me. The clairvoyant. Hanging out to dry here. Anybody listening?

"Nothing's happening." She covered her eyes, forgetting the ring was in her hand and sending it tumbling. Ryan found it and handed it to her.

She stuffed the ring into a pocket. Had her denial been so intense, for so many years, that she could no longer manifest visions?

What about seeing her grandmother's empty bedroom? Was that clairvoyance? Or was it her Nana's gift working through the magical cards?

Thoughts tumbled like confetti around her. Maybe she was Alice after all, and she'd walked through the looking glass.

How could her Nana let her think she was clairvoyant if she wasn't? Unless it was her grandmother's way to help a little girl cope with grief and loss. No. She'd been accepted into Harmswood Academy. She'd proven it to the admission committee. The gift was real; rusty, but real.

Ryan kissed her shoulder. "Where are you?"

His presence was like morning sunshine. At least he was very real and no dream.

"I'm not sure what to do," she said as she stood.

Ryan walked to her side, held her tight and gave her a loving deep kiss. Her giggle vibrated against his tongue.

"I meant about my future," she squeaked

around his lips.

"I know," he said as he kissed her again, and again.

In a way, she was glad nothing came through. She could go on being plain old Jess Callahan with a MIA grandmother. And a hot man's arms around her.

Hot? Jess pressed against his shoulders. "You smell that?"

"What?" He ran his finger over her chin and her lips.

A thrum coursed her body, but quickly halted. "Something's burning."

"I'm flattered," he said.

"No. Something really is burning." She poked a stick into the fire pit. Cold.

Was someone burning leaves? As dry as it had been, surely no one was that stupid.

Stronger, the odor scorched her nose. Then the vision.

A building consumed by a scorching fire. Windows exploded.

"It's our house." Her neck pulse galloped. How fast could fire trucks get here?

She broke away from Ryan and ran, slipping on flagstones and cursing her useless leather sandals. Bounding up the stairs, she burst through the rickety door, throwing it off its hinges.

Everything was fine.

With a sheepish grin, she went out to the porch where Ryan stood watching her; a woman who may have had a psychotic breakdown.

A stabbing pain shot through her temples.

Another vision.

Smoke thick as wool. Woods on fire. Crackling tinder. But where?

Her legs gave way. She dropped to her knees, engulfed in a burning firestorm.

"I can't breathe. Smoke. Everywhere."

"There's no smoke. What's happening to you?"

The animals. Screeching and howling. Panic. Fear. Trapped.

"It's the Sanctuary. Ryan, the fire is there."

Bewildered, he shook his head. "The Sanctuary

is thirty miles away."

Never a vision so powerful or so real. Not a hallucination. "Call somebody," she said.

"I'll prove it. I'll call Katya Dostoyevna. I'm sure everything's fine." He tapped in the number to the Sanctuary supervisor. Voicemail.

"It's not fine. I can see it. Disaster. Death. They'll all die." Tears ran down her cheeks.

"I need to get you to a doctor."

Her throat burned as she wheezed. "Not me. Save the animals."

"Believe her, Ryan."

Clear, distinct and loud, the voice belonged to Echo Stargazer.

"Nana? Help. Us. Please." Jess choked out the words.

Ryan looked around. "Where is she?"

"Do what I say. Go out there."

He turned his head, looking for Echo. "By the time I drive there—"

"Not drive, you fool. Fly."

"Tell me this isn't real," he said.

Jess struggled to stand. "It's real. You must go. I'll follow in the car." She turned away from him.

By some miracle, and Jess's stubborn perseverance, the 9-1-1 dispatcher agreed to route emergency units to the Sanctuary.

When she turned around, Ryan was gone.

"Thank you, Nana," she whispered.

CHAPTER TWENTY-ONE

Ryan circled the main building at the Sanctuary, darting through the rising smoke, looking for a safe place to land. Though only two fire vehicles had arrived, he couldn't risk being seen.

A few yards away from the access road, he landed in a recessed area in the bushes. Once he fully changed to human, he sat knees drawn to his forehead. Until the shifting effects wore off, he'd be no use.

How had he doubted, even for a minute, Jess's vision? While in flight, he'd witnessed the raging fire climbing the ridge as it approached the main buildings. He needed to tell someone.

He rose and stretched his arms, then made his way to a volunteer firefighter assembly point. He recognized them from Nocturne Falls. They'd believe his story about flying over the approaching fire.

As he explained what he'd seen, someone handed him goggles and pointed to a team wrestling a firehose. Ryan led them along a path toward the ridge.

Embers were floating in the air around them. If Jess was on her way, as he was sure she was, she better stay out of the way. This monster was gaining strength and moving fast.

Jess's forty-minute drive was nerve-wracking. All the while, an HD movie played in her head nearly blinding her. Flames lapped the Sanctuary perimeter. Pine trees burned like torches. Even her steering wheel burned like hot lava beneath her fingers.

Breathing became harder.

At the gate, just as in her visions, she watched fire plumes rise from the central compound.

Three fire trucks and a water tanker had arrived. Firefighters scrambled to run hoses.

But she couldn't see Ryan anywhere. With a falcon's speed, he had to be here.

She parked then raced toward the main building, only to be blocked by a state highway officer.

"Let me go in. I have to help." And find Ryan.

The patrolman insisted that she couldn't go closer. She stepped a few yards away and out of his eyesight.

Then she was overcome with another vision. A small nursery held the magical animals away from the public, hidden in the deep woods.

All the efforts were directed to the main building and beyond. There were no crews headed toward these woods. Smoke was growing thick; the radiating heat was everywhere.

With the bustle around her, Jess found the right

moment to run.

Following a narrow dirt path through the woods, she stopped three times to gag. Finding the strength, she pressed branches away from her until she came to a small clearing.

A few yards ahead, black smoke poured from a building. The nursery.

Her stomach wrenched. Anything inside might already be dead.

If she could get close, she might be able to see inside.

Before she could move, a wind gust rolled a dark cloud in her direction.

Retching again, she dropped to her knees. Any closer and she might die herself.

But there were living creatures inside. And though they were magical babies, they were helpless.

With one more gulp of air to fill her lungs, she crawled forward, feeling more than seeing her way to the building.

Single minded, she left fear behind.

Heat singed the hair on her bare arms. She blinked hard to clear her eyes and reached the door just as Katya came around the corner.

"Jess? Thank goodness it's you. Help me. This door. It's stuck."

Together, they threw their combined weight against the steel door as though they had any chance to open it.

She put her hand on Katya's shoulder. "Window?"

Katya led the way around the building and pointed to a small, high window just beyond her fingertips.

Jess found a brick and threw it through the glass, then motioned for a boost.

With a push from Katya, Jess scrabbled for a foothold and ran her hand along the sill until she found the latch. After sliding the frame open, she pulled herself up and through. Her feet steadied on a workbench, she hopped to the floor, then unlocked the deadbolt and opened the door.

The room lit only by smoke filtered sunlight,

the women went cage to cage. Was each one occupied? Where to start? The hot air nearly strangled her.

"Take these," Katya said.

A cage in each hand, Jess carried them far from the building. Katya followed with three smaller cages that she sat next to them.

No time to check which ones were alive or dead. They raced inside, the room filling with a dense, choking blanket.

Katya's emergency light shined an eerie glow on the terrified animals crouched in their cages. Some were leaning against others separated only by thin metal rungs, their eyes filled with panic.

Sympathy could come later. Now they had work to do. By Jess's count, there were still at least ten little creatures.

A long, frightening rip overhead caused both women to cower. "Ceiling," Katya said. "Move fast."

With two cages each, they raced to the outdoor holding area.

"How many more?" Jess asked.

Katya made a quick count. "Two."

"Stay here. I'll get them."

Inside the burning building, the ceiling had partially collapsed. Was she too late?

Just past the threshold, glowing beams blocked her. She willed a vision, praying this one didn't show dead animals.

The last two cages were on her right.

Her ankle turned as she kicked rubble aside. Just a few more steps. One more step.

Let them be alive.

The wire cages were hot to the touch. How could anything survive?

Despite the heat, she tucked one under each arm. To reassure the animals, and herself, she kept talking and fought her way to the door.

Though it scorched her throat, she forced herself to inhale desperate for any sliver of air.

Then she ran.

In the clearing, she and Katya loaded cages as fast as they could into a van.

THE FALCON FINDS HIS MATE

Once the truck was moving, Jess sunk into the passenger seat and wiped her arm over her eyes.

Through the thinning haze, they approached the triage area crowded with fire and rescue vehicles. After they had parked, she jumped out and gulped fresh air. Her nausea and dizziness eased.

Katya tended the animals then joined Jess. "They made it. They look like deer in the headlights, but they'll be okay. And you?"

Jess ran an internal scan. Throat raw. Eyes stinging. Blood running down her arm. White capris ruined. Urge to vomit waning. She was fine.

Jess hugged Katya. "We made it, didn't we?"

CHAPTER TWENTY-TWO

Jess poured water over her face and eyes. Her head still tipped to the side; she felt a hand on her shoulder. She stood and faced a man smeared with soot and dirt, dressed in filthy clothes and pitch black sneakers.

More soothing than water, gratitude washed over her. Ryan.

"I'm not sure who looks worse." His broad smile brightened his smudged face.

Her arms were around him before he could say another word. He smelled of burnt wood and ash, but no worse than she did. "You look amazing."

She hissed in pain as he brushed her arm. She'd

forgotten the glass cut.

"Crap. You're bleeding." He waited by the EMT truck while someone cleaned and bandaged Jess's wound.

Communication radios squawked. Another water truck crunched along the gravel road. Someone yelled orders to a group of firefighters.

Fire's stench everywhere.

She closed her eyes, waiting for another vision. This one came quickly.

In it, she floated above the trees.

White wisps circled over the hillside and around the main building.

No black smoke or glowing hotspots.

She lingered in her vision to be satisfied that what she saw was real and not her conjured imagination.

"It's under control," she said.

"What is?" Ryan squatted on the ground beside her.

"The fire. It's contained. They just don't realize it yet. And it's going to rain," she said. "Soon."

He scanned the cloudless sky.

She dug into her pocket for the ring and put it on. "Trust me," she said.

They leaned against her car while the fire crews reloaded equipment. The chief explained that one small contingency would stay behind to watch for any flare-ups, but they had a solid perimeter and firewall.

The Sanctuary was secured and except for the nursery which was a total loss, no damage that couldn't be cleaned up or repaired.

"Can I hitch a ride?"

Somehow Ryan's question struck her as insanely funny. A man who had shifted into the fastest bird on earth, and a first responder to a forest fire, needed a ride home?

"Can't you just wing it?"

He answered with an annoyed glare.

Jess nudged the car into the line winding down the access road. At the Interstate junction, most vehicles exited out of her way, and she picked up speed.

"You did a really foolish thing going into that building. You could have been hurt. Or died," he said.

"And we could have lost the animals."

"Still, a huge risk."

"Some things are worth the risk, Ryan."

Between adrenaline and sheer impulse, she'd pushed through broken glass and fire, uncertain what she'd find. Her possible death had only nipped the corners of what she had been compelled to do. Save lives.

She rolled the car to a gentle stop in the Carpe Diem driveway behind her grandmother's truck, still right where Echo had left it.

If Nana were here, little girl Jess would run inside and tell her all about her great adventure.

How she longed to hear Nana's tinkling bracelets as her grandmother smoothed her hair, and fussed about how proud she was.

And Nana would brew tea.

A gentle hand covered hers on the steering wheel.

"Car's still running," Ryan said.

She switched off the ignition. "What I did was crazy, wasn't it?"

"That nursery is hidden. The firefighters wouldn't have gotten there in time. Yes, you were crazy. A brave fool."

It had all moved so fast, too fast even to think.

Images replayed. Climbing through the window. Looking around the smoky room. The inferno. Carrying animals out, cage-by-cage.

His eyes were still fixed on her. His tender, loving, dark eyes.

"What now?" He asked.

"I'm filthy and need a bath."

"I mean about us."

Her hands grabbed the steering wheel again, nails pressed into her palms, the only way she could stop shaking. Staring forward, she couldn't bring herself to answer.

She knew what he meant.

The passenger door opened and shut. In her rearview mirror, she saw him walking toward his car parked on the street. No.

She threw open her door and raced down the driveway, breaking through a tourist family with children dressed as goblins.

One child called to his mother. "Look at that lady. She looks just like the guy over there. They're zombies. Cool."

Ryan stood beside his car, flashing a bright smile across a sooty face. Her heart unlocked as she ran to him. As she enveloped her arms around him, the words that wouldn't come earlier released in a flood.

"Don't leave like this. In the car, I couldn't think straight. My words froze. I still saw those poor animals. And you're right. I was a fool."

She rested her forehead against his chest. Though he still smelled of smoke, his embrace spread healing light through her.

"I'm curious. What happens if zombies kiss?" He asked.

"Huh?"

Ryan made a quick head nod toward the boy

who was still watching them. "Anything we can do to promote Nocturne Falls, right?"

"Ah. My thoughts exactly."

"That your only thought?"

His lips grazed hers in a gentle, in-public kiss, then released her.

"Not so fast, mister." Jess clasped her hands around his neck and pressed her lips into his. Their growing need was no match for the taste of smoke and ash.

"Eeeewe. They're kiiissssing. Yuck. They don't do that on TV," the zombie spotting kid said.

As rain began to fall, they broke apart but stayed in their embrace. The child's mother grabbed the boy's hand and mouthed 'sorry' as they rushed away.

"I'm not sorry, are you?" Ryan asked.

"Nope. But I was serious about a hot bath," she said.

"I suspect showering together is out."

"For now." But not forever.

CHAPTER TWENTY-THREE

A dinner date with Jess. Their second official date.

Ryan realized they had a lot to straighten out, but tonight, he hoped they might do a little more than talk.

He parked his truck in between the cars in his mother's driveway. Another gadfly party.

Before he could reach his door, Solange approached marching stiff as a general.

"We need you inside," she said.

Now what? "Who's we?"

"Don't pretend with me."

He knew whose cars those were, but facing her

shifter squadron was the last thing he needed.

"I don't have time. I've been busy, or haven't you heard? A fire nearly destroyed the Sanctuary," he said.

Typical Solange Ford prioritizing social niceties over tragedy.

"You have time. Come with me."

He could turn away, and suffer endless nagging, or get this behind him.

Her feathers were riled to let him inside her house looking like a rain-soaked 'zombie'.

Around a massive Louie the fifteenth dining table, ten women, each about Solange's age, sat with their sour faces focused on him.

Exhaustion had spilled the last drop of give-a-damn out of him. He'd play this to the hilt.

He bowed. "Ladies, my sincere apology for my appearance."

Solange took her place at the head. "No need for impudence."

To the person, no one broke her stare. Had they ever seen a grimy man before?

THE FALCON FINDS HIS MATE

This was a hopping mad gathering that could become a shift-con from hell.

His mother's crimson fingernails disappeared into her fists. He could almost hear her saying, 'all the better to claw you with.'

"Are you aware that you broke a cardinal rule?" Solange asked.

No kidding. He shifted before nightfall. Imagine the scandal.

"Yes."

"Not only could you be banished from Nocturne Falls; this could hurt us all," she said.

Banished? So be it. If Jess was with him, he could live anywhere.

The Ellingham's were strict, but not unreasonable. There'd be no repercussions.

The bigger question, how did these women find out?

"Who told you?" He looked from face-to-face hoping to see guilt flicker across a dowager's face. "Who saw me?"

His gaze circled the women until it locked on

his mother, whose hands had pulled to her lap.

"I'm the only person who'd suffer consequences," Ryan said. "There's no guilt by association in this town. Get Elenora Ellingham on the phone. I'll be delighted to tell her the whole story."

A collective gasp around the table was followed by mutterings. "No." "Don't do that." "Not necessary."

Somehow Solange had convinced these biddies to rally behind her. But why? She knew better than touting an Ellingham rule that could be broken in cases of dire need.

"What about your relationship with that woman?" Solange asked.

Bingo. There's her bottom line.

He splayed his fingers on the table and froze his stare on his mother. "Is this about Jess Callahan?"

In his peripheral vision, he could see the women exchange concerned looks. Then, one by one they made quiet apologies and left.

THE FALCON FINDS HIS MATE

After the last car door slammed and engine started, Ryan broke the silence.

"You were there," he said.

Solange walked to a window and opened the lace sheer. For a moment, he felt sorry for her.

Remembering how she'd deceived them into this confrontation, pity dissolved to anger.

He slammed his fist on the table. "You were there in the garden when I shifted." He persisted. "Weren't you?"

Ordinarily, he could sense shifters, in or out of human form. He'd been engrossed with Jess and let his guard down. "You were in falcon. Then you heard Echo's voice, too."

"I don't want you to get hurt."

"By what? By whom? How?"

"Jess isn't like us."

For that, he would be eternally grateful.

Salty pepperoni and triple cheese on a thick yeasty pizza crust had curative properties.

Not to mention the relaxed family-around-the-table antidote to the longest day on earth.

After his third slice, Ryan stretched and extended his legs under the table and his arms over his head.

Jess scanned his long torso. What would it be like to wake up each morning cuddled against this man?

Ding. Ding. Ding. What was she thinking? A kiss, or two, or three, wasn't the onramp to the full-out commitment highway. There were a few more complications.

"I'll get the dishes," he said. "You rest."

"Don't scrub too hard on those paper plates."

Ryan leaned close and nibbled her neck. "A light touch works every time."

Warm ripples moved from the crown of her head to her toes. Was she glowing like a lightning bug?

She settled into the two-seat sofa, one foot on either side of Crealde curled in the middle of the foot-stool.

THE FALCON FINDS HIS MATE

Still spooked by being in an empty house, at least Jess knew Nana would be there in an emergency.

But what was she going to do with this place? Or what she would do with the tall, dark, and handsome falcon-shifter in the kitchen.

How could she be sure if what grew between them was love, or lust that would fizzle after a few nights of wanton, crazed sex?

Ryan slid into the seat next to her.

Umm. Time to test her hypothesis. Her body quivered as his arm brushed across her. So close and available.

Then he withdrew his arm, the TV remote in his hand.

"Care if I turn this on?" He asked.

Mood killer. "Of course I don't." Much.

He flipped through channels until he found news coverage of the fire.

In a voice-over, the department commander explained that when they got the call about the Sanctuary, they were on the other side of the ridge.

They thought they'd contained the blaze but wind must have carried hot embers to the dry timber.

"I'm sorry for not believing you," Ryan said.

As the interview ended, the station ran video of the animals in a temporary holding area. Katya had spirited off the magical babies before the cameras arrived.

All the charged water in the world wouldn't disguise those to humans.

"What the hell?" Ryan shouted.

Jess jumped, her nerve endings still raw, as Crealde darted to another room.

He hit replay and froze an image, went to the TV and touched the screen on the roof above the animal holding pen. "I knew it. Dammit. She followed me. See? She's right there?"

"Who?"

"My mother."

Jess moved for a closer look. It was a bird. But how could he tell if it was a falcon? Specifically, a shifted Solange Ford.

Ryan hit play. Within seconds the bird took

flight.

"Are you sure?" She asked.

"We have to settle this, once and forever. And I need you with me. Up for a ride?"

After a day like this? She rubbed the bandage on her arm and stifled a yawn. Her throat still raw from the smoke, she answered, "Ready when you are."

Though she didn't think this was an invitation to ride to Nocturne Falls 'lover's lane.'

CHAPTER TWENTY-FOUR

With eccentricity the norm in Nocturne Falls, Jess thought she'd heard or seen almost everything.

But Ryan's story about the Inquisition at his mother's shifter council ranked at the top.

Solange had sunk to an all-time low. Yes, her son had broken a rule, but to save lives. Living in the Ellingham community meant following certain standards, but they weren't oppressive.

They were meant for the community good and to protect the supers. Where else could a person like her grandmother live in peace and raise a reluctant clairvoyant grandchild?

If Jess hadn't seen the fire, those animals would

have died in agony. Bile rose in her throat. That second pizza slice may have been one too many.

She looked at her jade ring. It might be a long time before she took it off again. But a little heads-up about what was going to happen between Solange and Ryan would be helpful.

After parking, he came around to the passenger side. "This could get dicey. Think you can handle it?"

Dicey drama with Solange Ford? She placed her hand in his and squeezed. "Oh, hell yes."

"Mother, we need to see you," Ryan announced as he and Jess walked through the front door. After a few seconds of silence, he repeated, louder, "I know you're home."

"No need to raise your voice." Dressed in a silk caftan and a bath towel wrapped around her head, Solange descended the stairs like an old film star walking toward a camera close-up.

His cold glare at his mother counterbalanced the laugh rolling up from Jess's toes. Something was different about the woman.

Then she got it. Solange didn't have on any makeup. Without it, she looked pale and out-and-out peaked. And ten years older.

Ryan's long fingers enclosed Jess's hand. Pity any prey caught by a shifted falcon's talons.

"You were there," he said.

Solange completed her descent and waved her hand at them. "Perhaps."

"Knock it off. I saw you on the news footage," he said.

Solange bristled. Then the sharp-tongued queen of mean started a faux collapse. Ryan caught her in mid-slide. "Okay. Showtime's over."

Solange opened one eye and cocked her head at him, brushed her son's arms away and stood straight and tall.

"Anyone for tea?" She said in a cheerful voice as she walked toward the kitchen.

Ryan slipped his arm around Jess's waist. "I think Merlot might be better."

"I have an Oregon 2005 I've been dying to open," Solange said.

Jess mouthed 'is she for real?'

He nodded and winked.

They sat at a granite breakfast bar in the enormous kitchen. "Sit down, ladies. I'll take care of this," he said.

His impeccable sommelier skills were impressive and the wine was delightful. After this short intermission, Jess was ready for the next act.

Solange swirled her wine glass. "Perhaps it's time I explained."

Ryan stood across from both women, tapping his fingers on the counter.

"You and Connor mean the world to me. And I want nothing more than to see you happy and successful." Solange's voice poised on the diving board but didn't jump into the sincerity pool.

"We got that." Ryan drank his wine without moving his eyes from his mother. "What's that got to do with spying on us, then following me to the Sanctuary?"

"I wasn't spying. I was going to plead one last time for you not to get involved with her. With

Jess."

Reality check. A deep quaking shook Jess's bones. "That broken limb that fell between us was you, wasn't it? I can't believe you'd try to hurt us."

Solange's eyes opened wide. "I'd never do that. Please believe me. It was a complete accident. I misjudged that tree. I might be getting too old for this flying thing. I did follow you to the Sanctuary. I was so afraid for you."

"Then you went home and called the crones. Nice move," he said. "And thanks for all the help."

Jess waited for a safe opening. "Solange, Ryan and I have a lot to think about. All we ask is that you respect our wishes and give us privacy and space."

Though Solange remained silent and possibly indifferent, Jess at least had her say.

Solange tented her fingers. After several moments, she spoke in a voice just above a whisper. "Your father wasn't my first love."

Ryan's wine glass hit the granite but somehow didn't break.

THE FALCON FINDS HIS MATE

What in the name of all this Earth did she just say? Jess made a slow head turn to the woman next to her.

Solange just hit a fly ball out of the park. Only this one kept sailing. It might hit the ground somewhere in Tennessee.

"When I was your age, I fell in love with someone who wasn't like us," Solange said.

Make that landing place Ohio.

Jess took the wine bottle and filled her glass double the dab that Ryan had poured. The 'not like us' story was about to roll.

Solange waited for a rise from her son. Not getting one, she proceeded.

"He was a wolf shifter from another community. A wonderful looking man. Intelligent. Caring. Even if he was a bit on the wild side."

"I don't need to hear this," he said.

"But you do. You must understand why I know how you feel. And how Connor felt with his past girlfriends. Remember, we falcons mate for life. You must make the right choice. Someone who understands us."

"We can marry outside our own. Especially today." He stared at Jess. "There are no boundaries around love."

Taking another drink, Jess was still dealing with how to love a shifter and didn't want to read too much into what he said.

"His pack leaders forbade it, so we planned to elope. We were going to Atlanta and be married in secret. But they found out," Solange said.

"How could they stop you?" Ryan's voice dropped a pitch.

"He and I planned to meet at a spot in the forest. I got there first. He was nowhere around.

But his mother was, and as a menacing and evil wolf. I can still feel her hot breath on my legs. See the spittle hanging from her jaws.

After circling me, she shifted into human. She told me that I had to be the one to break it off; say I didn't love him. Otherwise, she'd have him killed."

"Holy, hell," he said.

Solange continued. "His was a mountain pack

that was nearly feral. That's what drew me to him. But, I also knew they wouldn't bat an eye to kill their own to maintain what they considered pack purity.

I couldn't live with myself if I was the reason he died. So, I did what she asked. I found him and told him I didn't love him."

Jess laid her hand on Solange's arm. "But you did love him, didn't you?"

"To this day." Solange's eyes searched Ryan's face. "I also loved your father, deeply. He was my mate. He knew what he walked into from the beginning.

But we made an excellent life together. You and Connor were the joys in our lives, and still are in mine. Though Connor fuels my migraines."

The room fell into an unyielding quiet except for the refrigerator's hum. Jess released Solange's hand. Drawn into an intimate conversation between a mother and her grown son, she should excuse herself.

The wine had hit her. Her muscles screamed.

She needed to get off this stiff barstool, but she dared not move.

Solange dropped her head into her hands. "I've become like that she-wolf, haven't I?"

"Connor and I can't stay under wing our whole lives," he said, the sharpness gone in his voice.

With her haughtiness dissipating, Solange faced Jess. "You're not a shifter. How can you know what it's like to be half human? And not knowing in which world we belong."

Not belonging was something Jess knew all too well. It's why she loved Boston where you could disappear into the crowd. No one cared who, or what, you were.

No one cared about you at all.

"Have you ever watched my son shift?"

Solange's question stabbed Jess's soul. Watching him shift meant accepting his falcon side.

"I have not." Her answer came from a deep well.

The bigger question, could she?

THE FALCON FINDS HIS MATE

The rain slowed to a drizzled on the drive to Carpe Diem. "I'll walk you to the door," Ryan said.

"I'll be okay. You need sleep. You have a lot to think about." For a fact, she certainly did. Solange Ford's confession had left her brain scrambled.

"You want me to go?" he asked.

Tell him 'no'. Draw him to her arms. Take him upstairs to her bed and make mad love all night.

Instead, she said, "I need time."

Without answering, he gave her a soft, warm kiss. And then another, this one more loving.

Their lips parted as he whispered, "Take all the time you need. Just remember this."

He pulled her close for a third kiss, much more demanding.

One she would always remember.

She knew he wanted more, as did she. But Solange's words resonated as she eased away from him. 'Have you ever seen my son shift?'

What would happen when she watched this

handsome, hundred percent, human man, turn into a born-to-kill falcon?

CHAPTER TWENTY-FIVE

Light beams played a hiding game between the tall pines and splashed over Jess, seated on a rock near the falls, wrapped in the tweed jacket Ryan had left behind at Harmswood gym.

Arms folded around her knees, she stared into a pool below. The break in the heat signaled early fall. There was solace in this peaceful place, swathed in the sound of the waterfall and rustling squirrels burying acorns.

Ryan and Jess had agreed to take time apart to consider their future, and to meet at this spot today.

Though she longed to see him, Jess's mind had been in a continuous problem parade. She'd finally decided that the expedient thing would be to sell the Carpe Diem and take the new job a thousand miles away from Nocturne Falls.

A leaf turned in lazy circles in an eddy below. Without warning, the unsuspecting sprig spiraled into a vortex, spinning against a force that compelled it toward oblivion.

Fed by nostalgia, and perhaps a liberal dose of 'I'll show you', she had jumped feet first into her own spinning water.

With only herself to blame, she managed to splash into Nocturne Falls with a vengeance.

Solange's revelations forced both to face the truth. A shifter and a psychic couldn't be any happier than a leaf spinning to its own demise.

Two squirrels scampered around a tree beside her, disappearing into the branches. Like with like.

A sudden warmth flooded over her, spreading from head to toes, covering her in bliss and erasing her fears.

Another rustle above, followed by the sound of wings. Anticipation and terror commingled with the tingling buzz throughout her body.

"Ryan, it's okay. Come down beside me."

Something landed nearby, but she continued staring at the waterfall. Could she bear to see him as an animal?

Would she freak? And if the sight repulsed her, would that destroy him?

If he left in humiliation, the pain she caused him would stay buried inside her forever. It can't end this way. They will part in dignity, not in disgust or shame.

Eyes closed, she turned, quarter inch by quarter inch only opening them when she was sure she faced him.

Her breath caught. His feathers, a blend of dark and light browns, overlapped in soft tones and hues, except for one stray wing feather that stuck out from the others. Just as unruly as his hair.

The dark piercing eyes that had bore into her soul as Ryan Ford stared at her as a stately falcon.

Ashamed that she'd been afraid to see him shifted, she wished she could find the right words.

Or, any words. Her mouth opened but her throat was paralyzed.

The falcon dipped his head. He understood. The unspoken question hovered between them.

And then she had the answer. "I'm ready."

A glowing aura surrounded the falcon and she couldn't pull her eyes away from the transformation into a full-grown man dressed in flannel and denim.

She licked her dry lips and swallowed the lump in her throat. "Well, you certainly know how to make a grand entrance."

"There's my jacket. I wondered where I left it." Ryan managed a watchful smile. "At least you didn't run."

No. She hadn't. Nor considered it.

More than ever, she wanted his strong arms around her again. She did belong somewhere. Here. With him. She would never leave his side. Or Nocturne Falls, or give up Carpe Diem. She was home.

She bolted toward him, then stopped. What if he'd changed his mind?

No way could that happen.

"We'd save time here if you'd kiss me," she said.

Pulling her into a tight hug, he nearly squeezed the last ounce of air from her lungs. "Hey." The word muffled into his chest. "I. Said. Kiss."

His lips playfully nibbled down her neck. "Are you sure?"

"Never more about anything in my life. Ryan Ford, I love you."

"Even though you see what I am?"

"But, I already know what you are. A strong, creative, considerate being that I will love until time ends."

Something flew overhead. Surely that woman hadn't nosed into their privacy again.

Ryan's chest tensed against hers.

If this was how that busy-body Solange planned to carry out her mother-in-law role, she had another thing coming.

Something caught Jess's eye as it floated to the ground beside them.

"A feather?"

His face beamed. "From Mother. She won't bother us again. Except advice on decorating the nursery. She loves a tidy nest."

Jess's laughter rose over the forest hush. "I'm all for a few concessions. Just not green walls. I don't like green."

"I'll make a note. Now, future mate, may I give you a proper kiss?"

"Proper is not exactly what I see in our immediate future."

Jess slipped off the jacket, laid it on the soft leaf bed, and gently pulled him down beside her.

"And just what do you see?" He asked.

Her kiss was all the answer he needed.

THE END

THE FALCON TAMES THE PSYCHIC

CANDACE COLT

THE FALCON TAMES THE PSYCHIC

Brianna Putnam needs a juicy scandal and fast. Up for a promotion at a high-profile tabloid, she has one month to convince a hard-nosed editor that she has the chops for the job. What could be better than a story exposing Nocturne Falls, a town full of supernatural beings? She has the perfect cover. Her grandmother and her cousin are self-proclaimed psychics who live there. No time like the present to meet the family.

Play-boy falcon-shifter Connor Ford is filthy rich with nowhere to be and nothing to do. About to give up on finding his life's purpose, he meets Brianna, and his passion ignites for the beautiful woman with the strange curiosity about his hometown. When he discovers she's played everyone for fools, Connor arranges a surprise to turn the tables on her.

Finally accepting her psychic gift, Brianna is overcome by guilt after submitting the story. When her editor arrives to see the town for himself, she has a chance to redeem herself. But will it be too late?

CONTENTS

CHAPTER ONE

Who on this planet would ever paint a house bubble gum pink?

Brianna Putnam leaned on her rental car and tapped her sunglasses on her lips. If the GPS was accurate, the three-story Victorian looming in front of her was the Carpe Diem. Though the flying pig weathervane indicated North straight ahead, she knew she faced East.

Somebody should fix that.

A pint-sized Jack Sparrow whirled by, but not before jamming his little black boot on Brianna's sandaled toes. Hopping on one foot, she massaged the other as she sliced a 'gee-that's-okay' grin to the wild child's apologetic parents.

No sooner had that troupe gone on their merry way, along ambled two adults dressed in fringy B-western cowboy outfits.

Wasn't the first week in October a little early for trick-or-treating?

She glanced over her shoulder as a tram chugged past and choked back laughter as the guide pointed out highlights.

Highlights indeed. Brianna had heard nothing but lowlights about Nocturne Falls all her life from her father.

She doubted tourists would hear his version of a town full of eccentric looney tunes who honestly believed they were supernatural beings passing themselves off as normal humans.

As children, Brianna and her brother Samuel made their father retell his stories over and over. Awestruck about a town where every scary creature imaginable lived and breathed, they'd begged him to bring them here.

Each time he vehemently refused. And to this

day, he had never explained why.

If there was more to Nocturne Falls than cute storefronts, then a juicy exposé would get her a front-page story. Best of all, she'd graduate from copy editor at La Grande Bouche tabloid to feature article writer. A headline on page one.

And the raise would give her enough money to get an apartment of her own. She could only dream of the day when she'd have a private bathroom.

Sharing an LA apartment with four other women had stretched her tolerance to hair thin. One consistently left the sink in chaos. One borrowed anyone's deodorant. And one always used the closest toothbrush.

All Brianna had to do was wheedle her way into this town and snoop. But with every step to the Carpe Diem's front door, her heart raced faster until she thought it would leap from her chest.

Playing this undercover game seemed easy when she first hatched the idea. But pull it off for a whole month? If she wanted this story, she would. Maybe no one else believed she could do it, but she knew she could. It had taken some high-powered convincing to get this assignment, and she wasn't about to fail.

Just one little barrier.

The owner of this building that looked like it was right out of a Tim Burton movie was Echo Stargazer. The same person her father had warned Brianna and her brother about all their lives.

His mother. And Brianna's grandmother.

She slid her sunglasses on top of her head, smoothed her skirt, and marched up the steps to the front door.

She gulped, shut her eyes, and gripped the door handle. Then she saw the sign. 'Temporarily closed. Re-opening on October 20th.'

This jimmied her plans all to heck. Nothing online said the place was closed. October 20th was three weeks away. Her entry point into the town was meeting Echo. A solid Plan A.

There was no Plan B.

Confident a brilliant idea would eventually come to her, Brianna followed the wrap around porch to the side of the old house, every footstep creaking on the weathered wood. Some might say this added charm. To Brianna, this place looked like a house flipper's dream.

There was a quaintness to it, though. And a real old-fashioned wooden porch swing.

She ran her hand up the heavy chain. From how old it looked, no doubt her father had sat here as a kid.

Who'd notice if she swung in it for a few minutes? For sure, her pirate-stomped foot would be happy. Though her toes barely touched the floor, she managed to rock the swing.

She relaxed a bit and glanced around the neighborhood, likely the same as when her father lived here.

Maybe smaller back then, the trees were probably here, too. A sudden gust of wind swirled leaves around her feet. She picked up an amber one that had lifted in the air and landed beside her.

As she ran her finger around its ruffled edge, she considered sending her father a quick photo of the old house.

What would that accomplish? He had nothing good to say about the town. Besides, he didn't know she was here. If he found out, he'd go off the rails.

"It's not open."

Shaken from nostalgia, Brianna searched for the voice's owner. On the driveway behind her stood a man in a filthy T-shirt and jeans, and a backward ball cap.

With hands on his hips, he glared at her. Must be the lawn man or caretaker.

She stood a little too quickly, and the swing slapped the back of her knees sending her wonky-legged.

"Sorry." Why was she apologizing to a man who for all she knew was a burglar?

Cripes. Maybe he was, and she'd interrupted him in the middle of a break-in. "Can I help you?" He asked, a bit more agitated.

Well, after all, she had taken her sweet time to answer. And would a burglar strike up a conversation?

"Uh. No. Actually. I was about to leave. I was checking phone messages." Right. Sure. Sitting on a stranger's porch swing checking messages. This was not going well.

He removed the cap and wiped his brow. Maybe he was hired help, but he certainly had a to-die-for body. Those arms were about to burst through his shirt. His tight abs met his waistline like an old friend and his jeans hugged him in all the right spots.

Good grief. Pull it together. Long flight from LA and drive from Atlanta. Long day all around.

"There are more shops downtown." His voice had the edge of a weary guard-dog.

"I heard so much about this shop. I'm disappointed," she said.

"Sorry. Can't help you. Like I said, more places up the street."

Though he acted like a troll guarding his bridge, he was far from a wart covered hobgoblin.

She hadn't traveled this far without at least peeking at the place where her father lived.

"Okay if I walk around outside?"

He turned and stared with the most remarkable blue eyes. Sharp eyes that made her feel like a one-inch-high moron.

"It's just a yard. Nothing special," he said. "But I guess it's okay."

She darted her glance along the edge of the driveway and noticed blooming chamomile and lavender. "I love herbs. Are there more in the back?"

He held his hands open toward her. "Probably. The owner is famous for herb teas. It's kind of overgrown so stay on the path and be careful."

The meandering cobblestones were bordered by an unkempt hedge encroached with leggy plants. Instinctively, she broke off several distressed sections from a rosemary bush, releasing its delightful savory scent.

A few steps later she spotted a tiny lemon balm sprig strangling in a weed vine. She pulled the invader away from the herb. "Now, that's better," she whispered. "Wish I had time for some of your soothing tea."

At the end of the path was a small fire pit. Brianna kicked a rotted limb out of the way and dusted leaves from the benches that circled the pit.

If there was such a thing as an enchanted garden, then this was it. Or, it could be.

It took weeks for a garden to fall into disarray, and it would take weeks to bring it back to life. But with care and know-how, the place would be spectacular. Just like her mother's rose and herb garden at home.

Do roses even grow in this part of Georgia?

If this was her grandmother's garden, why would she let it get this bad? Was she ill? Was that why the place was closed?

She hadn't come to this town for garden restoration. If nothing else, the brambly mess gave her clues that there was more here than met the eye.

She wound her way back to the run-down building where backward-cap man had disappeared.

Brianna poked her head inside. The place was packed to the rafters with boxes, dilapidated furniture; even an old jon boat. Dust drifted like fog.

Fighting a sneeze, she shouted, "Hello, again."

Wearing earbuds and with his back to her, he apparently didn't hear. "Sir," she said louder.

Startled, he swung around and bumped an old dresser. The box he carried dropped from his hands and the contents scattered.

"Let me help." Brianna bent over and scooped what she could to refill the box.

"Don't bother." He squatted beside her. "I got this."

As they reached at the same time, his long leg connected with hers causing her to fall flat on her butt.

Hells bells. This was class-A bad.

The man gripped her forearms and effortlessly brought her to standing as though she was a down pillow. "Are you okay?"

If mortified counted in the 'okay' column, then no she wasn't. Good grief, he was strong. Those arms and pecs weren't for show.

Calm down, woman. Not the place or time for desire bumps to show themselves.

"I'm sorry about the mess," she said.

He snuffed a laugh and gestured around the building. "You and me both. Can you tell I've been hauling stuff out of here for two days?"

Not her place to say it, but what did it look like before? Overrun like the garden?

The sneeze she'd bottled exploded, followed by two more brain rattlers.

"Bless you," he said.

She could use some blessings this month.

"I'm Brianna."

"Connor."

He offered her a firm, gentle handshake without a trace of callouses.

She was a little disappointed when he finally released his grip.

While Connor went back to work, Brianna's eye caught on an old photo that had escaped the box and landed on the ground in front of her. She started to toss it back, but something compelled her to take another look at it.

Faded after years stored away, it was unmistakably a little boy eight or nine years old with a flat-top buzzed haircut, wearing baggy shorts and a plaid shirt.

So much like the few pictures her father had saved. This had to be him.

She waited until Connor turned away, then she stuffed it into her pocket to study later.

She wiped a sweat bead from her temple. This building was stifling.

"Couldn't you find someone to help you?" Argh. She'd done it again. She'd lifted the filter between her big mouth and nosy monkey mind.

"It's not that hard, and I don't have anything else to do. I may go home and throw out everything I own. That minimalist thing sounds good to me right now. Like this, for instance." He tossed a tennis ball-sized snow globe up in the air and caught it. "Why would anybody keep this?"

Brianna loved snow globes and at last count, she had twenty-two. Most were in her parent's basement in Oregon, but she'd brought a few with her to LA.

Watching the swirling snow always calmed her, but wasn't nearly as much fun as shaking the daylights out of it first.

"May I see it?" She asked.

He shrugged and handed it to her. "Keep it if you want. Next stop is the dump, anyway."

This globe was made with a real glass ball, not cheap plastic. Brianna scraped some unidentified dried crud off the side, then turned it end over end. Once it had been a funky little souvenir that had entertained its owner for a few moments, or perhaps a few years, then joined the legion of the lost.

Had it belonged to her father? Or maybe it was just something that didn't sell in this Carpe Diem store. One day she'd settle down in her own place, and this little globe would find a home with all her others.

Right now, settling down seemed a hundred light years away.

Connor reached into a cooler and took out two

bottles of water. He offered one to Brianna, opened the other and took a long drink.

On the label: 'Moonbow Water. Locally Bottled from the Falls.' Interesting.

And it tasted like the Oregon mountain water she loved. Almost sweet. Pure and clean. None of that LA chemical tap water brew.

"I should be leaving. Sorry if I bothered you." She scanned the building. "Good luck with your project."

It seemed he needed more than luck.

As she walked by his truck, she scratched the head of a huge white cat resting on the hood. "Aren't you a pretty one. And such a good kitty to stay up there and out of the way. I love your eyes."

CHAPTER TWO

Connor Ford halted in his tracks; his eyes glued to the shapely backside of the petite curly-headed blonde walking down the driveway.

Impossible. Completely and totally. It did not happen. He did not see it. He was exhausted. Overworked. Hallucinating.

Unimpressed as usual, Crealde the cat stretched and yawned, spun in a circle and went back to sleep.

Connor had watched Brianna drink at least half the Moonbow water; more than enough to block a human from sensing supernatural beings.

Then how the heck was she able to see the obese and totally invisible Crealde?

THE FALCON TAMES THE PSYCHIC

The woman was a looker, no doubt about it. Those ruby red lips matched her painted toes, and that skimpy red dress barely covered important aspects of her anatomy.

Maybe she was a tourist dressing like Marilyn Monroe. He'd seen a few of those around here, though none pulled it off quite this well.

He'd squelched a laugh when she dropped to the floor like a stringless marionette. She was so light that he almost pulled her into his arms as he lifted her. *Almost* would have been *absolute* for the old Connor Ford.

Turning a new leaf sucked.

Connor 2.0 had made huge inroads toward better behavior. He had learned more lessons in the past weeks than in all his four years at the University of Georgia.

By any standards, those had been the lost years. He'd made terrific friends. Dated knock-down stunning women. Played football; second string but still on the team.

He'd kept the party going when he moved to

Atlanta after college. Then last year, his father died and Connor's mother, Solange, expected him to come home and take on a larger role in the family business.

Looming over his head like a Damocles sword had been the understanding that he and his brother Ryan would marry into a high-society family.

Fortunately, the Ford Financial Group's senior team kept the company moving forward, though there were rumors of a takeover and an ouster of his mother as a principal partner.

So, he partied on, until everything changed.

Connor still couldn't decide what had surprised him more.

His brother's choice of a human mate? His mother's blessing? Or his future sister-in-law's decision to marry a falcon-shifter?

Once his big bro took that leap off the branch, Connor did the unthinkable.

He backed off from his wild lifestyle, though he was a long way from a rocking chair in front of a roaring fire.

THE FALCON TAMES THE PSYCHIC

Dancing all night at the Insomnia bar didn't appeal to him half as much as it once had. Sleeping until two in the afternoon then pumping iron for two hours didn't cut it. Getting comfortable with himself had been a new adventure.

Right now, his priority was learning about Connor.

He'd wasted years trying to find a mate that met his mother's standards. In the future when it came time to choose, it might be a shifter. It might not. And on his terms and no one else's.

But this Brianna woman who wandered in from nowhere, and who saw Crealde was a mystery. He should have asked more questions, starting with her last name. Why was she so troubled about the Carpe Diem? There were other places to spend money. What was that whole walk around thing about?

He had way more to do than ruminate on a stranger, attractive or not.

He'd promised to have this building cleared out before his brother Ryan returned from Boston. He'd be done if he hadn't put it off for two weeks. Not everything about the old Connor had changed, yet.

Now, with less than six days to go, this monster mess got worse by the minute. For every ten truck loads he hauled away, twenty seemed to refill the place.

If he didn't know better, he was sure the damn sprites had something to do with it. It had been a long, long time since they'd singled him out, but this had all the earmarks of their old game.

He shoved a box into the last available niche in the truck bed, then pulled a tarp over the whole jumbled pile. Before locking the building, Connor took a photo of the contents then waved the phone in an arc.

"For the record, don't even think about putting anything else in this truck, or anything back in that building. Got it?"

Even though he was a shifter living in a magical town, he had no real way to back up a threat to his unseen nemesis. They didn't need to know that.

It was worth the effort to put a little scare into

them.

Minutes after unlocking the door to her room at the Gingerbread Inn, and without bothering to unpack, Brianna undressed, tossed her clothes on the bed and went straight to the shower. Savoring every sweet moment, she let the hot water run through her hair and down her back.

For a whole month, she wouldn't worry about borrower roommates.

After towel drying and slipping into a pair of jeans and a blouse, she sat cross-legged on the chenille bedspread and examined the little photo. It had to be her father. Behind him was the building where she'd found the picture, and the same little footpath that she'd followed, though the plants looked much healthier.

The child held the serious no-nonsense look that her father always wore.

Brianna wondered who took this picture. His mother? Was it for a special occasion? And why wasn't his little sister in the picture?

She tucked it into her portfolio then turned her attention to the snow globe.

Almost worn away on the base were the words, Souvenir of Nocturne Falls. Inside was a painted miniature rock falls. Brianna tipped it over, then upright, taking care with this one as she wasn't sure how old it was.

Mesmerized, she watched the tiny flakes float to the bottom. Then something weird caught her eye.

No.

She shook her head. She was more tired than she realized. She put it on the bed stand and unpacked. But the globe drew her like a magnet. No indication that it was battery-operated. Just a simple snow globe and not a nightlight.

She tipped it over and waited.

As sure as sunrise, water flowed over the falls.

It had to be lighting effects on the paint. It was too old to be a computer toy. Something else had to explain it.

THE FALCON TAMES THE PSYCHIC

She held the globe up to the waning sunlight through the window.

As she predicted, nothing moved inside it. Imagination again. Must be triggered by her hunger.

Time to grab something to eat and explore the town. After a good night's sleep, she'd rethink a plan B. Or was it plan C at this point?

Too bad Echo Stargazer wasn't here. She'd like to meet her. But that meant everyone would know who Brianna was. It would be easier to snoop around if nobody knew.

There was a story here somewhere. It was up to her to crack it wide open.

CHAPTER THREE

Big Daddy Bones barbeque was a touch of heaven on a checked tablecloth.

Sometimes eating alone in a restaurant had its advantages. Brianna jumped head first into her meal with no concerns about that date-politeness and baby-bird appetite stuff.

The ribs were so tender they fell off the bone. The loaded baked potato dribbled sour cream and butter. Brianna didn't care what anyone thought. She ate that baby, crispy peel and all. And a side of fresh green beans with a touch of ham hock was divine.

The Gingerbread Inn proprietor's restaurant

recommendation had been spot on.

LA indulged every foodie whim on the planet, and local eateries in Portland were outstanding. But nothing compared to this meal, except everything that came from her mother's kitchen.

Food this good always prompted her to try her hand at cooking. Thankfully, the thought always passed before causing any long-lasting commitments to the kitchen.

As the server cleared the table, she offered a dessert menu.

"I couldn't eat another bite." Somewhat true. She could chow down on a slice of peach cobbler if she was so inclined. But her expanding waistline disinclined. Tomorrow she'd find a running trail.

Dusk faded into night and the streetlights turned the already quaint town into a wonderland. With illuminated storefronts and people everywhere dressed in costumes, the whole town held an aura of fantasy.

Funny how her father had never mentioned any of this. She was tempted to go inside every store and start asking questions, but not on the first night. She'd use this evening to get a feel for the town.

She crossed the main square bordered by giant concrete gargoyles and could have taken an oath in court that one of them winked at her.

Another impossibility. She turned back once for a double-take, but the stone statue stared forward, unmoving.

Ahead was a sign for The Poisoned Apple. What a stitch. Everything in town had the cutest name.

A glass of Chardonnay meant another half-mile added to her next run. Who cared?

Inside, the pub had an old-fashioned tavern atmosphere with its dark paneling, deep green paint, and luscious leather upholstery. Rather than sit in a booth, she chose a seat at the bar.

As she sipped the pleasing, fruity wine, she asked a few subtle questions of the bartender but didn't get deep, revealing answers. Perhaps the townspeople knew better than to say anything that would tip off a stranger.

THE FALCON TAMES THE PSYCHIC

She'd have to be crafty to work this story. The 'gee-golly-gosh-I'm-family' card would be the last one she'd play. If she got this right, she might even open the door to her father's heart.

The sober little boy staring out from that photo still dug under her skin. A smile from him was rare and hard won, even today.

She scooted her barstool a little to allow room for someone to sit next to her. The scent of bay rum cologne wafted her way. Not overpowering. Just nice. Pretending to focus on her phone, she cast a slant eye stare at the man.

Nice khakis. A form fitting T-shirt hugged a toned torso.

"Evening, Brianna. Anyone sitting here?"

Connor from the Carpe Diem? She didn't mind, though there were other free stools at the bar. The bartender placed a pint of stout in front of him without a word. He must be a regular.

"Hello," she said.

Connor offered another handshake. Surprised at how gentle his grip was, she was pleased at how he lingered this time. Mr. Backward Hat had disappeared. This was one classy maintenance man.

She snuck a quick look at her chest. Oh, great. A fine time for the girls to snap to attention. And a bad idea to wear a gauzy top. Tightening her arms to her sides, she clasped her hands together on the bar.

"Everything going okay so far?" His soft-spoken, deep voice was pleasant, and much friendlier than before. What did she expect earlier? After all, she had overplayed the role of nosy tourist.

"Yes. I'm staying at the Gingerbread Inn. It's quite nice." Brainless dodo. Never tell a strange guy at a bar where you're staying. What was she thinking?

"Good choice. I'm Connor Ford. I don't believe I caught your full name."

His piercing eyes sharpened. He might be hitting on her, though she doubted it. Either he was genuinely nice, or she was under the spell of a half-glass of wine.

THE FALCON TAMES THE PSYCHIC

What the heck. Why not tell him her real name? No one around here likely knew her family anymore, especially someone young like Connor.

Her grandmother, Echo, had changed her last name to Stargazer. Brianna's father and his sister left town a long time ago.

"Brianna Putnam." There. She said it and he didn't seem shocked or alarmed.

"Sorry if I sounded rude earlier," he said.

"I guess it seemed pretty bold to sit on the porch swing."

Connor glanced over his shoulder and down the line of people seated at the bar. He must be waiting for someone. Wonder what type of woman he dated? He seemed the long, lean brunette type.

And not short and less-than-lean blondes.

She squeezed her curls. "If you need this seat when they get here, I'm leaving soon," she said.

His eyebrows raised as his head cocked to one side. "When who gets here?"

"I just thought. Aren't you looking for someone?" She touched her lips to the rim of her glass but didn't take a drink fearing she'd choke on the wine.

"Not me. Thought maybe you were," he said.

She finished the sip and sure enough, the liquid went down the wrong pipe.

"Are you okay?" He asked.

She nodded as she coughed.

"Raise both arms over your head. That clears it every time," he said.

Ah, not such a good idea in this blouse. "Maybe…some…water?"

Connor motioned to the bartender. A few sips and Brianna was fine.

"Are you on vacation?" Connor asked.

"Yes. A friend told me about this town."

"What do you think so far?"

"From what I can tell, it's interesting."

His hearty laugh was infectious but all she managed in return was a weak smile.

"Good word to describe it," he said.

"Have you lived here long?"

"My whole life."

Her first lead. Now to weave in some subtle questions.

"I've never seen or heard about a place like this, outside a theme park. Is it like this all year?" She asked.

"You mean Halloween? Twenty-four seven. Three sixty-four." He sipped his beer. "I've never understood why so many people flock here."

Spoken like a true townie. He might prove to be an excellent ally.

"So, if you're from here, I guess you know everyone," she said.

He nodded and motioned his empty glass to the bartender.

"Would you like another glass of wine? On me," Connor said.

Brianna rarely had more than one, but she felt like she had him on a roll and didn't want to lose the momentum. If she drank water between sips of wine she should be okay.

Letting him pay didn't seem fair. He obviously worked hard for his money.

"Yes, but I'll get my own," she said.

Ian, the bartender, shot Connor a wide-eyed 'are you kidding?'

Connor returned a silent warning not to go there. It was a rare day for a Nocturne Falls woman to buy her own drink when he was around. This woman obviously wasn't from here.

Kind of nice for a change.

The bigger puzzle was why an attractive woman was sitting alone.

An hour later and finished with her second glass of wine, Brianna hadn't told him anything more than she lived in LA and was here on vacation.

No denying that Nocturne Falls was a great place for tourists. But a world-class singles' travel destination? Not-so-much.

Of course, Connor had a way of talking more than listening. Maybe his constant voice overs didn't give her a chance.

THE FALCON TAMES THE PSYCHIC

About to give up on her, he remembered how Crealde was as real to her as this pint of stout on the bar. Only a supernatural could see that invisible behemoth cat.

"I should be going. It's been a long day," she said.

"Any questions about the town I might answer?"

She paused a moment and turned her head toward him giving him an opportunity to see her gorgeous big blue eyes.

"Is there someplace where I might learn more history? Travel sites don't give much detail other than restaurants and places to stay," she said.

Imagine that. Nothing on the Internet about the vampire family that founded the town? Or the beautiful mermaid he dated once. Or the exotic fortune teller at the hair salon. Or the falcon-shifter Ford family.

"There's a library," he said.

After she had left, Connor ordered another pint. Ian took Brianna's empty glass and wiped the bar. Under a wad of napkins, he retrieved a silver infinity bracelet. "Before you got here, she had this thing going like a fidget toy. She's one spooky chick."

Connor sputtered into his glass as he laughed. Spooky chicks abounded here, and Ian had seen his share.

"How was this one different?" Connor asked.

"A barrage of questions about the Carpe Diem. And she asked about Echo Stargazer like she was a concerned friend. She wanted to know if Echo was sick. Seemed strange but maybe it's just me."

"Maybe."

Why didn't Connor drop this? She was a curious tourist on vacation and would be gone in a few days. But this fascination with the Carpe Diem was peculiar, especially since Echo had disappeared two months ago.

"Something else." Ian leaned toward Connor. "I didn't think much about it at the time. Thought it was a coincidence. I pulled a back muscle last night hauling kegs."

"And?"

"She asked if I'd tried a cold pack on it."

"What's wrong with that? Good advice."

"I never said anything about my back."

Brianna leaned on the headboard and braced her laptop computer on her thighs. With a light buzz from the wine, she'd almost floated along the sidewalk.

The bedside lamp bathed the room with a homey glow. Lace curtains, overstuffed pink upholstered chair, and the white enameled armoire made her feel like a princess in one of her favorite stories.

All she needed was a knight in shining armor.

Sleep seduced her, but she had to submit her daily report, a condition of getting this assignment. Aside from wandering around her grandmother's weedy garden, having a fantastic meal and meeting Connor Ford, there wasn't more to say.

Usually able to figure out a man soon after

meeting him, and especially after one drink, this one was an enigma. Dressed like a maintenance man before, then this evening like he was ready to party. Probably one of those who lived for quitting time so he could head out with his buddies.

He seemed nice but he wasn't much help about Nocturne Falls, aside from suggesting the library. Connor had yammered more about his brother's woodworking than anything personal.

She held the photo and stared into the little boy's face looking for anything that explained his dark memories of Nocturne Falls. And maybe something that might help her understand his obsessive protection of his children.

Part of it was over his daughter's health. Brianna had missed half of first grade with recurring headaches. For a solid year, she lived wondering when they would hit. Her head would burn like fire. Then the disturbing thoughts and thinking she heard people talking to her.

She'd had brain scan after scan. No physical answers. She'd even been to a child psychiatrist who confirmed she was a normal little kid. How were debilitating headaches normal?

Then the week of Brianna's eighth birthday, a small package arrived in the mail from her grandmother, Echo Stargazer. Her parents had argued over letting her open it, but her mother won.

Under a layer of brown wrapping paper, Brianna discovered a small, pink jewelry box with a shiny silver bracelet. Inscribed on the inside, *Forever in My Heart.*

It had fit her tiny wrist perfectly, and with each growth spurt, the bracelet somehow adjusted.

And the sick headaches disappeared, along with the voices.

Traveling, time changes and the wine had caught up with her. The Chardonnay's pleasant lightness was quickly being replaced with the first twinges of a headache.

Instinctively, she gripped her wrist, bolted upright, and shoved her sleep shirt sleeve up to her elbow. Throwing back the down comforter, she ran her hand over the mattress and under the pillow.

On her hands and knees, she looked under the bed.

Retracing her steps to the bathroom, she scanned the floor, dresser, and sink counter.

She dumped her purse on the bed and sifted through the contents.

The bracelet was gone.

CHAPTER FOUR

"I'm sorry Miss Putnam, but nobody's turned in anything like that," the Inn's proprietor said the next morning. 'I'll call Big Daddy's. Bet they have it.'

"I had it on after dinner. You don't need to call the restaurant."

"How'd you know that's what I was going to do?"

The dumbfounded expression the proprietor wore was the same as the bartender's when she suggested a cold pack on his back.

Hadn't these people spoken to her?

Or had these been voices in her head?

Was it starting all over?

Brianna grabbed an espresso at the Hallowed Bean hoping it would knock out her roaring headache.

Her boss's answer to her quick report last night had been terse and to the point. 'Get more.'

That meant a long day digging into library resources and interviewing anyone who walked across her path. No time for pain or phantom voices.

She'd walked right past the Inn's attractive array of breakfast foods, none of which appealed to Brianna's queasy stomach.

Nor did an investigation into this little town in North Georgia. What had she been thinking? Was a job promotion in a tabloid run by an editor that reminded her of a wild bull, worth the effort?

She'd put her career on the line chasing after her father's bitter memories.

Besides, that photo might not even be her father. What if she'd agonized for the last eighteen hours over a picture of someone else?

THE FALCON TAMES THE PSYCHIC

"Hold your horses." Connor went inside the kitchen where Crealde sat at attention amid cat food cans he'd knocked to the floor, howling in a relentless '*I-am-starving*' siren.

"Did you think I'd forget to feed you?"

Crealde turned and raised his tail, flashing his bottom toward Connor.

"Keep that up and see what you get." How could one cat be so egocentric to think nothing in the world meant more than a filled dish?

Connor restacked the food tins on the counter, then decided to put them in a corner on the kitchen floor, where they'd land anyway.

"Buddy, what would you like this morning? A nice liver pâté? Chunks of beef in gravy?"

A can slid across the floor and careened off Connor's foot. "Guess it's ocean fish day."

Connor held his breath and spooned the fishy goop into the dish. Crealde pushed his head between Connor's feet and immediately began scarfing down the unappetizing gumbo.

"Bon appétit."

Though he'd only been in the Carpe Diem a few times before he agreed to house sit, Connor remembered how noisy and busy the place always was. Except for Crealde's meal-slurping in the kitchen, the tomb-like quiet in the building was unnerving.

After her sudden departure for what she called a 'time travel adventure,' Echo had turned the building and business over to his brother's fiancé, Jess Callahan.

Connor had no doubt Jess could handle it. There were few women like her and Ryan had been darn lucky to get her. Though gifted with clairvoyance, Jess was still human. Putting up with a falcon-shifter husband would be a full-time job by itself.

At least it would be for Connor's mate.

Crealde jumped up by the sink and enjoyed a post-breakfast tongue bath while Connor rinsed the cat's food dish.

THE FALCON TAMES THE PSYCHIC

He looked out the window at Echo's pickup truck and its tarp-covered load.

The latest trip to the dump would be two hours out of his life that he would never get back. No big deal.

He'd already chalked up all these care-taker duties as a portion of the penance he owed to the universe. If he helped every old lady he saw cross the street for the next ten years, it wouldn't make up for his reckless past life.

But he didn't regret a minute of it.

"Crealde, I think it's time we get this day going."

With a *flaumph*, the cat dropped to the floor and waddled to the screen door. He rose on his back feet, stretched a front paw to catch a claw in the handle, and then opened it.

Before Connor caught it, the door banged shut nearly smacking the cat on its behind.

"Damn it, Crealde. I wish you'd stop that."

But why would a cat give a flip that most everyone in Nocturne Falls had superhuman hearing, and every loud noise drove them up a wall?

Wonder how Brianna was feeling today? She'd downed that wine like a pro, but as small as she was, it might prove a mistake this morning.

Ian was right. She was a little spooky, and just the type who'd have a great time in a library; a place he'd rarely visited.

Connor doubted she'd find anything exciting among the dusty files. The real Nocturne Falls story wasn't written anywhere.

Thanks to the Ellinghams' foresight, this old town had found a new life. Without a place like this to live and prosper, his family would have been screwed.

He checked the tie downs on the truck and crossed his fingers. When he got to the dump, he better find it was a load of junk.

The last time, everything he'd loaded had been returned to the building and the truck bed was full of leaves and branches.

Damn those sprites or whoever they were.

That was another thing. Brianna had cherished

that old snow globe like it was gold. Whatever. To each their own.

Of course, Nocturne Falls was spic-and-span clean this morning. Not a paper or straw on the streets. And not her bracelet.

Espresso and two pain pills had reduced Brianna's raging headache to a hum. But it was still there, thunking away on her skull as she scanned every nook and cranny on the sidewalk.

She'd worn that bracelet for almost eighteen years, taking it off so rarely that she forgot when the last time was. All those years just to lose it here?

And those voices. Jumbled and indistinct, they filled her head. Half sentences. Half thoughts.

Hallucinations had held hands with her severe migraines. She remembered how awful these were when she was a kid.

Were they back?

Wheels on the sidewalk caught her attention.

"Good morning." A cheerful voice called from

behind. Or at least she thought it was a real voice.

Thank goodness. It was the bartender from The Poisoned Apple.

He hopped off his skateboard and walked alongside her. "Glad I found you. I think you left something behind last night."

"My bracelet?" Of course. That's where she'd taken it off, sometime during the first glass of wine, for no good reason, other than nerves.

"I'm on my way there now. It's in our lost and found."

Someone drove by and honked, sending a shockwave through Brianna's skull. She turned to the street and recognized the old pickup truck from the Carpe Diem. Connor, backward hat in place, hoisted his arm in a salute out the window of the muffler-challenged truck.

Ian waved and yelled back, right into her ear. Stereo sound explosions.

She tossed back the last of her coffee, happy that the pub was only a half-block further.

"That's it." Brianna slid the silver bangle on

her arm. "Thank goodness." Moments later, the tight band strangling her head for the last nine hours was gone. She'd been stressing more than she thought.

She thanked Ian and explained that not many people in an LA bar would be this honest.

"That's the way we are here. I'd have brought it to you, but I didn't know where you were staying," he said.

"I'm just happy to have it back. It was a present from my grandmother." She averted his gaze. She'd almost said Echo's name.

"Hope you enjoy your day," he said.

Indeed, she would. Outside, she glanced at the clock in the town square. The Gingerbread Inn still offered breakfast for another hour, and she was starving.

On the way back from the landfill, Connor stopped at the Ford estate to inventory his brother's tools and supplies. If the sprites left him alone, he'd have that building cleared out and ready for his brother's studio with only one or two more trips. He hoped.

He was surprised to find his mother, Solange, inside the studio. Arms folded across her chest, she leaned on the back-door frame looking out to the pine trees bordering the property perimeter.

"Made your decision?" She asked without turning around.

"I have." He had his eye on a one-bedroom cottage not far from the Carpe Diem, with enough room for his weight machine and a carport for his Porsche.

He hadn't driven his baby for two weeks. Echo's pickup was fine for hauling trash but didn't have much highway jazz.

"I hate the thought of living here alone," she said.

Connor knew what was next. The poor me song. He wouldn't feed into it. Not today. "You know what I think you should do."

"I won't sell." She turned to Connor, her face

dark with worry. "Your father and I came to this town with nothing. We built this place. We raised both of you here." She walked to the threshold leading to the driveway. "And he died in that house."

Even more reason to pack up and move, if you asked Connor. If cleaning out Echo's shed took loads of dumpster trips, he shuddered to think about emptying a five-bedroom house. His mother could hire someone for that.

The ceiling in here was higher but the new location had more floor space. The collaboration of Jess's carpentry skills and Ryan's design ideas would turn an old shed into a showcase.

And not a minute too soon. Ryan's client orders came in from all over the world.

A few weeks ago, Connor took his brother's place and flew on a private jet to deliver a commissioned carved stallion to Dubai. Connor had never been prouder of his brother than when he witnessed the new owner's delight.

Ryan Ford had found his niche. He had the love

of his life. He was happy.

Connor Ford glanced at his reflection in a wall mirror. In a sleeveless t-shirt, holey jeans, and greasy cap, he stared at a man with an uncertain future.

He made an overhead press with a three-foot section of an oak tree trunk that Ryan had started carving. If he had his way, Connor would buy a fitness center and work out all day.

"The board of directors is going into special session at the end of the month," Solange said.

Connor's arms weakened, and he dropped the wood on the concrete floor.

"Why?" He looked for any dings or nicks. The last thing he needed to do was ruin Ryan's next commissioned piece.

"It's been almost a year since your father died. They're ready to install a permanent Chairman," Solange said.

"You think they're still planning a hostile takeover?"

"Our attorneys do. But I think we can still win

the majority."

Who's this *we*? Ryan had no interest and Connor didn't know enough to be dangerous about corporate operations. And Solange had left decision making to her late husband.

"How do you propose that happens?" He asked.

Three inches taller than Connor, Solange was an imposing sight at a distance, let alone as she walked toward him.

She placed her hand on Connor's unshaven cheek.

"I have an idea," she said.

Her icy words poured over him and triggered his sudden urge to shift and escape on the wind.

CHAPTER FIVE

Fueled on a cinnamon crunch sweet roll, peach compote, fresh yogurt, and two glasses of hand-squeezed orange juice, Brianna worked straight through lunch and into the late afternoon. The Nocturne Falls public library had tons of history resources, and the librarian had been delighted to provide her with anything they had, no questions asked.

More than once a twinge of regret plucked Brianna's heartstrings. No matter what she found, she'd made up her mind that she'd tell the truth about this town. So far, she hadn't found a single shred of diabolic scandal.

THE FALCON TAMES THE PSYCHIC

A family named Ellingham had rescued the little down-and-out town and rebuilt it into a tourist destination. The community embraced the concept of Halloween all year-round. There were monthly festivals and celebrations.

Schools and shops just as anywhere else. A local newspaper. Hair salon. Bakery.

All the trappings of small town USA.

All cozy and sweet.

Perhaps too cozy and too sweet.

Brianna needed to burn off energy and clear her head. She had time to walk back to the B&B, change and get a good three-mile run in before dusk. The break would do her good.

She ran along a gentle rolling trail that led through beautiful woods. The crisp late autumn air invigorated her, though she could only manage a slow jog around the families with baby strollers, kids on skates, dog walkers, and bicyclists.

A blessing in disguise, this forced her to slow down and absorb the natural beauty around her. There were places in Oregon near her parents' home that were like this. In June when the roses were in full bloom, Portland was the most beautiful place on earth. But this part of the world was a close second.

A few yards ahead, she stopped at a bench to stretch her legs.

Down a few feet from the bench was a stream flowing over flat rocks. A fat squirrel, oblivious to the intrusion of people around him, munched on a prized acorn.

Her city-wise hackles skittered up her back as she sensed someone approaching from behind. She dropped her foot to the ground, prepared to run.

"Brianna?"

She jerked to attention. "Connor?"

"Sorry if I startled you. Didn't expect to see you out here." Shirtless and glistening with sweat, Connor's chest heaved as he caught his breath. He worked out and from the look of his six-pack, a lot.

He stretched his arms overhead and to the sides allowing her a wonderful view of the elaborately tattooed wings that capped each shoulder.

As he flexed his arms, the wings seemed to

come alive.

She battled with her desire to run her hands over those wings, and other places.

"I love running, and this trail is awesome," she said.

"Running keeps me sane," Connor said. "So, which way you headed?"

She looked around and realized there were fewer people than before. The sun had dropped behind the trees casting long shadows.

"I should get back to the Inn."

"Mind some company? It's safe out here, but since you're new, you might not be used to it."

They fell into a comfortable jog, side by side. Soon they were the only ones on the trail, and the only sounds were their footsteps and their breath.

The path seemed longer going back, and much lonelier. Typical for her, she'd ventured out farther than she realized. She glanced over at the strong man running next to her.

It was a relief having him at her side. He was right about not being used to this place.

Her mind was messing with her. Twice she imagined something stared at her from the trees.

She glanced down at her silver bracelet. She couldn't blame every irrational thought on the migraines.

Up ahead was another bench and a water fountain.

"Can we stop a minute? I'm thirsty," she said.

Connor pressed the fountain button for her while she drank the fresh, cold water. As she wiped her hand across her lips, she realized he was staring off into the trees and hadn't let go of the fountain button.

He did a quick double take, noticed she was done and took a drink himself, then stared back to the woods.

"What is it?" She asked in a hushed voice. If only she had her pepper spray.

"Nothing. Ready to go?"

Would *nothing* cause a man's arm muscles to clench?

A pair of bicyclists raced past, laughing as they

pedaled ahead. Good news. They weren't alone out here. She didn't fear Connor, but she sensed he didn't like what he saw in the trees.

They ran in silence for the next fifteen minutes until they reached the town. She felt a little out of place running along the sidewalk with Connor, but much safer.

In front of the Inn, she thanked him for coming along with her and apologized if he went far out of his way, all the time unsuccessfully prying her eyes away from his body.

"Not a problem. I'm staying upstairs over the Carpe Diem until the owners come back. Maybe I'll see you again?"

Upstairs over the Carpe Diem? Oh, yes, he would see her again. And soon.

Connor sprinted up the back steps to the apartment, where Crealde sat squarely in front of the door, his tail wrapped around his front feet.

"So, I'm fifteen minutes late. Sue me." After

unlocking the door, Connor attempted to nudge the cat to the side. When Crealde wouldn't budge, Connor stepped over him and into the kitchen. "I await your dinner choice, your royal *catness*."

While Connor dripped sweat in the middle of the kitchen, Crealde slowly tapped his nose along the top of each food can, finally stopping at the seafood medley.

"Your wish is my obligation." Connor opened the tin and dropped the blob into the cat dish, then shook his head in bitter disgust at the smell.

This was one lucky animal.

In what parallel universe would a falcon become a cat's manservant?

He peeled off his running shorts and tossed them and his socks into the washer, then padded naked through the apartment toward his bathroom.

As he rounded the corner from the kitchen, he plowed his thigh into the dining room table.

"There's no room to walk through this damn place," he yelled.

"I beg your pardon?"

THE FALCON TAMES THE PSYCHIC

Connor grabbed a placemat off the table and covered his privates the best he could. "What the hell?"

"Don't let me interrupt your shower plans. I can wait."

"*Who* can wait?" Connor's eyes darted around the room. "*Who* are you?"

Crealde jumped on the table and shifted his body side to side as though rubbing on something.

Connor scooted behind an overstuffed chair.

"I looked inside the shed. You've done a great job cleaning it out. Sorry there was so much. I can't resist new things, nor can I throw out anything."

"Echo," Connor whispered.

"Go take your shower. I can't stay long and I need to talk to you. Fully dressed might be more appropriate."

Heat bloomed on his neck and circled his ears. "I need to get to the door. Mind turning your head?" That is if she had a head to turn in this state.

"I most certainly have a head, young man. And I can still read your mind so be careful. Now skedaddle."

Placemat installed as a frontal cover-up, he backed his way into the bathroom. On the counter were a fresh pair of underwear, a T-shirt, and shorts.

How did she do that?

He raced through the shower, dressed in the clothes laid out for him, and came back to the dining room. A plate of his favorite rigatoni and sausage, a hot garlic roll, and a glass of peach ice tea waited for him.

"Now then. Have a seat. Enjoy your meal," she said.

The initial shock had faded, replaced by a ravenous appetite stimulated by the glorious aroma of Italian spices, though he had no idea how the food got there.

"Home delivery from Guillermo's," she said. "I put the bill on your tab."

He sniffed a laugh then bit off a chunk of the garlicky roll. "If I'm supposed to carry on a conversation with you, would you mind mentioning if you're standing or sitting, and where?"

THE FALCON TAMES THE PSYCHIC

"Sitting right across from you, sweetie."

There was no trace of anyone there, but if that's where she was, she was.

"I wasn't spying on you in the woods earlier. But I think you can guess who it was," she said.

"Mother?"

"Bingo."

"I will never understand her. What's her problem?" Connor asked.

"My opinion? I suspect she's worried about you and that new woman."

Did Echo know everything?

"Not everything, sweetie. Remember, sometimes it's a lucky guess."

"So, what brings you back? Or should I say *halfway* back?"

"Don't get cute, Connor. If there's an emergency, it's always possible. Do you remember it was an invisible me who kicked your brother in the behind to fly out to the Sanctuary the day of the fire? But, I must say, it's challenging to jump forward from the seventeenth century. So, it was much easier for me to leave my body back there."

Connor opened his mouth to say something clever but thought twice. There were more important questions that needed answers. Why did she leave? And why's she here now? Why not wait till Jess comes back?

"It's complicated, Connor."

He bet the bank that was right.

CHAPTER SIX

Talking to a mind reader's disembodied voice was surprisingly easy, once Connor got over the 'no body' issue.

He circled his plate with a piece of garlic bread to sop up the last of the marinara sauce.

Cannoli would be a nice touch.

"Don't push your luck," Echo said.

"So why here and why me?" Connor pushed his plate away.

"Like your mother, I'm worried about the new woman."

Brianna Putnam. The nosy little blonde.

"Yes, her," Echo said.

"Would it be easier if I spoke all my thoughts out loud? It might save some lag time."

"Sorry. I left my blocking bracelet back there. If you don't mind me saying, I never knew your mind was so noisy."

"In a minute, you might want to turn the channel," Connor said.

"Let's get to the point. I need your help."

"My help?"

Crealde raised his hindquarters as Echo's unseen hand scratched his back.

"I sensed something's going on with this woman. That's why I'm back. Whatever she's up to isn't good for Nocturne Falls. I don't think she wants to do it. Something or someone's put pressure on her."

"She can see Crealde and she reads thoughts," Connor said.

"I'm aware."

"So why don't you hang around and listen in?" Connor took his dishes to the kitchen.

"That silver bracelet blocks her ability to hear

thoughts, and when she has it on, it blocks my ability to hear hers. This is going to take more than my gift."

How did Echo know about the bracelet?

"I gave it to her," Echo said.

The fork and knife fell from Connor's soapy hands and tumbled into the sink. He walked back into the dining room, still wiping his hands on a towel.

He stared at the empty chair and the unseen person with whom he'd been talking to for the past forty minutes.

In any place except this town, everything that had happened inside this room would make a case for his swift committal to psychiatric rehab. There was still an outside chance he was crazy as a pet 'possum.

"Echo what did you just say?"

"You heard me. I gave her that bracelet. Oh, not directly; I mailed it to her. Somehow my daughter-in-law convinced my pig-headed son to allow her to have it. I knew Brianna had the gift.

Her father knew it, too. But he's still in denial."

"Wait. That means—"

"Brianna's my granddaughter. Her father and I don't get along. Once he left Nocturne Falls, we never had any further contact. That was over thirty years ago."

Connor didn't get this at all, nor why he was privy to a family secret. But at least it explained why Brianna saw the cat and how she read thoughts. And why she was so nosy about the Carpe Diem.

"She needs to discover that Nocturne Falls is a decent place filled with decent people. She needs a strong person, and a good friend, to find out what's eating her," Echo said.

"You can't mean me?"

"None other, sweetie."

Crealde jumped off the table and headed to the door for one last trip outside for the night.

"I'll let him out," Echo said. "You think about what I told you. Ciao."

Echo and the cat disappeared into the night.

Which one would return first?

THE FALCON TAMES THE PSYCHIC

CHAPTER SEVEN

If Brianna had tried, she couldn't have picked a worse place in the entire Nocturne Falls library to concentrate on a pile of books.

The window overlooked a peaceful courtyard of brick paths, benches, and archways of flowering plants. Beyond was a thick stand of trees.

All of it beckoned like an ancient siren.

Her windowless cubicle at La Grande Bouche minimized distractions. Just as the editor wanted it.

All he cared about was turning out the stories and generating more revenue.

But here, after every other page or two, the compelling view hijacked her attention. Such a beautiful day and here she sat, glued to a chair going through old historical library records.

Brianna didn't want to hurt the librarian's feelings after he'd combed the collection to find these for her. But this was the most boring project ever.

And the deadline loomed.

What's the use of plowing through the rest of this stuff? She hadn't found anything new. She'd try one final document, a small business directory, then head out on the town.

She scanned down the index. The same names appeared that she'd seen before.

Until she hit on one that stood out like a beacon in a storm.

Solange and John Ford, primaries in Ford Financial Group, or FFG. Associates, Ryan and Connor.

Connor Ford?

With renewed energy, Brianna ran a computer search for Ford Financial Group.

The company's net worth was more than the

GDP of a small country.

Now she had a lead. A real lead.

A half hour later and with a file full of information on the Fords, she shut her laptop and turned her attention to the squirrel in the courtyard.

None of what she'd read made sense. Why would a family that ranked among the richest in the southeast live in this small town in the Georgia mountains? They could live anywhere they wanted. Sure, it was a cute place, but isolated.

Her father had never mentioned the Fords. Perhaps they came to town after he left. Or, had their wealth been part of his resentment?

Her father didn't talk about why his widowed mother brought her two little kids here, but Brianna suspected Echo didn't make a lot of money running a gift shop.

This assignment had shifted gears. How had a quick and dirty tabloid story deepened into finding the truth about her family? Too bad Echo wasn't around. Brianna would love to meet this woman and find the real scoops, or at least hear her side.

THE FALCON TAMES THE PSYCHIC

As for Mr. Connor Ford, she'd be darn sure he'd buy her a drink next time.

Connor waited a distance away from Brianna, seated at a study table. Surrounded by books, folders, and her laptop, she looked like an adorable college student studying for finals.

If Echo was right, Brianna wasn't cramming for a history test unless it was Nocturne Falls history.

He needed an excuse to be here and a strategy to get the answers he needed without raising her suspicions.

He sat down at her table, clasped his hands, and leaned forward.

"Hi, Brianna."

Though she managed a pleasant 'hello,' everything about her shouted 'what the hell are you doing here?' He deserved that. "Finding what you need?"

A smile edged across her red lips. She didn't

look a thing like her cousin Jess, but he didn't look like his brother Ryan, either.

She nervously scooped the materials into a pile, away from his side of the table.

He snuck a glance at them as she shut her computer. On top was the city directory. Guess she knew who he was now.

"Anything I can answer?" He asked.

She seemed to relax as she thought a moment. "How is it that most small rural towns are nearly broke, but this one's thriving?"

"It wasn't before the Ellinghams took over. After that, people started moving in and opening businesses."

"From what I read it was a ghost town."

"You could say that." *And now it's a vampire, shifter, fairy, mermaid, pick-your-supernatural town.*

She continued her line of questions. If Connor didn't know better, he'd think her interest in Nocturne Falls was genuine. After what Echo said, he doubted it.

He picked up one of the musty old books. "There's a better way than this. I'll treat you to lunch then give you the grand tour."

After lunch at Mummy's Diner, they walked up and down Main Street, going inside stores and meeting townspeople.

He watched her sharp edge mellow. It didn't seem fake to him, but she might be a good actor.

He'd met his share of players and thanks to his mother, almost married one.

If he ever became serious about a woman, it would be on his terms. A falcon mates for life and he'd rather be alone forever than suffer in a miserable mother-induced match.

Falcon mate choices in Nocturne Falls were slim. Not zero yet, but approaching. Though his playboy game had faded, Connor's reputation still followed him and not every suitable woman wanted anything to do with him.

Unless he devised a good alternative, which seemed unlikely, he might soon be running the family business. Real work gave him heartburn.

But, it might be his ticket out of town and back to Atlanta, and a whole new pool of available women.

Before his father died, Connor didn't give a hoot about Ford Financial Group as long as he had his monthly allowance. Now there was a strong possibility that he'd lead the entire corporation. What he wouldn't give for more time to mentor under his father.

What good did it serve to look back? Not one damn bit.

They stopped at the Hallowed Bean for coffee and took their drinks to a shady spot outside. Brianna sipped some frothy concoction, while Connor drank an espresso.

"I've been thinking, and I still can't understand why so many people visit here. Once they've wandered around and shopped, what's left to do?" She asked.

A line of creamy froth coated her upper lip, drawing him to her red lips. He pretended interest in three pigeons pecking at crumbs on the ground.

THE FALCON TAMES THE PSYCHIC

He glanced back as she ran her tongue over those lips. Was she deliberately tempting him? Or was she one of those naturally sexy chicks who had no idea how attractive they were?

He shut his eyes and finished his espresso.

"People come here for the same reasons some go to theme parks. They get caught up in the magic." Connor tossed his empty paper cup in the trash. "And where else can grown adults play dress up in the middle of the day, and nobody pays attention."

"Do you ever wear costumes?"

"In second grade I was a knight." After he'd discovered his ability to shift into a falcon, playing dress-up didn't mean much.

"A knight? Really?" She poked her straw in her drink. "Mind if I ask what you do, that is beside hauling trash?"

Her question stung like being hit with a two-by-four. "What I do?"

Her silver-dollar-sized eyes locked on his. "I doubt cleaning out sheds is your full-time job."

Full-time job. There's a joke. How did he spend his days? Two hours on the weight machine. At least a five-mile run. Drive too fast. Annoy his brother. Shift into falcon when the mood struck. And until a few weeks ago, party the night away downtown.

Next day. Sleep. Eat. Repeat.

"Our family owns a business."

CHAPTER EIGHT

It wasn't much to go on, but it seemed Brianna had finally cracked Connor's reluctance to talk about himself.

No wonder. Why would he share with a stranger that he was filthy rich? The Fords had been a part of this town since the Ellinghams revitalized it. Perhaps they helped orchestrate this whole Nocturne Falls scheme.

Connor hadn't taken his eyes off Brianna for the last five minutes and hadn't said another word.

She misjudged the distance to the straw and winced as it jammed into the top of her mouth.

He reached a hesitant hand toward her. "Are

you all right?"

With her tongue flat on the roof of her mouth, she mumbled, "Yeth. I'mth finth."

Embarrassed all to heck, but fine.

"If you're up to it, there are more places I'd like to show you," Connor said. "Or maybe you need some down time?"

Not a chance she'd go back to her room, now. She had a deadline and Connor was the only lead she had so far. She'd endure.

"Let's keep walking," she said.

By four o'clock, they'd been inside every store and met every shop keeper, and passed more kids in space travel costumes than she thought ever existed.

Brianna's feet were screaming by the time they reached the Carpe Diem. But Connor seemed to have endless energy.

"I don't think I can go another block," she said.

"I figured that. You've seen almost everything else, but I thought you might like to see inside the store."

"I thought it was closed?"

THE FALCON TAMES THE PSYCHIC

"It is. The owners won't mind," Connor said.

The empty porch swing easily rocked in the breeze. She imagined what it would be like if her grandmother were in it waiting for her. Would they even recognize each other?

Brianna walked inside the store and stopped in her tracks. Had she walked into a Halloween-R-Us store?

Shelves were loaded with knickknacks; pumpkins, black cats, cauldrons, spooky caricatures, scrying tools, crystals. And that was just in the first few feet inside the store.

After a long exhale, she managed, "Ohhhh my goodness."

Connor laughed as he removed his sunglasses. "Now you see why I saved this place for last?" His brilliant blue eyes twinkled.

"I don't believe this."

The store where her father had grown up and from the looks of it, remained untouched all these years. Cobwebs in the corners. Paint peeling.

Either it was part of the creepy Halloween

theme, or her grandmother hadn't gotten around to a fresh coat of paint.

Either way, Brianna wondered if she'd wandered into a time capsule. She didn't get a vibe that this was the typical imported junk store.

Composed, she took a self-guided tour and realized the place wasn't a helter-skelter shop at all. There was a definite organization, though the average person might not see it.

Further in the back were ritual materials. Herbs, cauldrons, athames, candles, incense. A Wicca superstore. She had friends who would die to see this.

"What do you think?" Connor asked.

"I love it." She was drawn to a shelf where crystal and stone pendant necklaces hung on a rack. As she brushed her hands under them, they began vibrating. Was there a draft in here?

She looked around, but nothing else moved, except Connor who'd been leaning on a doorframe but now stood tall and stiff. His expression hardened.

She pulled her hand away wondering if she'd done something wrong.

"You know what pendulums are, right?" Connor asked.

"Things that swing inside a clock?"

He tipped his head and stared at her.

"No. Seriously," she said. "What are these swinging things?"

"Run your hand under them again. This time slow. See what happens."

Sounded foolish, but he seemed so serious about this that she tried it. She brushed her hand under the pendulums and they started vibrating just as before. Small vibrations turned to stronger ones.

One crystal almost jumped from the stand.

She pulled her hand back and grabbed her wrists behind her. "Did you do that? Did you flip a switch or something?"

Connor shook his head while he removed the chain with the crystal and showed her how to hold it, so the point was over her open palm.

"Hold the chain right where my hand is," he

said.

She slipped her hand over his, hesitating a moment while she gave him a quick smile. Slowly he withdrew his hand from under hers.

He then guided her other hand so that her palm was inches away from the crystal.

"Stay still and wait," he said.

She scanned his face for any hint that this was a prank. If it wasn't a joke, and he truly thought something was about to happen, she had more concerns than ever.

"Exactly what am I waiting for?" She asked.

He didn't answer. Instead, he kept his eyes on the dangling pendulum. This was getting scary. Alone in this store with a guy playing games.

"See?" He asked.

Brianna cast a slant eye to the pendulum. It vibrated as before, but this time faster.

Ridiculous. Connor had talked her into thinking something was happening. She rolled her eyes to the ceiling. She'd had about enough.

"Brianna," Connor began in a low tone. "Look

at your hand."

She huffed a breath and reluctantly watched her palm. Her skin was warming up and a hint of an image appeared.

Her stomach cartwheeled. "Connor, what's going on?"

The pendulum made slow figure eights over her palm until an infinity symbol appeared.

Infinity? Like her bracelet?

The chain slipped through her hands, and the crystal hit the wooden floor, spun and slid under a cabinet. Neither one spoke as the image faded.

Connor took her hands in his.

"Brianna Putnam, we need to talk."

Her heart thumped inside her chest like a war drum. "What I need is to sit down."

"There's an apartment upstairs." Connor's smile went a long way toward calming her nerves. "We can talk there."

Chintz and pink everywhere, down to the appliances, walls and kitchen curtains, the apartment seemed like an oversized doll house. And no way suited to the hunky Connor Ford.

He filled her crystal glass with ice water, then sat across from her at the kitchen table.

"Okay, what was that all about down there? A trick?" She rubbed her fingers across her palm where the lighted symbol had been. "A hologram?"

"Not a trick, Brianna."

Crealde hopped on the table between them. As Brianna petted him, the cat's purr grew to the roar of a Blackhawk helicopter. When he'd had enough, he flopped on his side and fell asleep.

"He's a sweetie, but man what a voice. Those blue and green eyes are captivating," she said.

"What I'm about to tell you isn't going to sound rational, but will you promise to hear me out?"

Brianna screwed her mouth into a question mark. What possibly required this much preamble?

Whatever it was, her chances of landing the money-story were rising like the sun.

She took a long drink of water. "Go ahead."

"You've never been to Nocturne Falls before,

right?"

She nodded.

"Never met Echo Stargazer?"

She shook her head. Nor had she ever seen the woman's photo.

"What happened downstairs only happens to people with a special psychic gift. I've heard people talk about the infinity sign. Believe me. It is real."

That was completely nuts. The town was full of delusional people, just as her father had said all along. Too bad this gorgeous man across from her was part of the loony bird club.

If she played along, she might get more dirt.

"You think I have a magical gift?"

"Yes. I suspect that's one reason you came here, isn't it?"

She didn't want to lie but she couldn't tell him the truth, either.

Crealde chose this moment to jump down, catching his claws on the table cloth. As he whipped his paws to release them, his tail hooked her water glass.

Connor and Brianna's hands met on the crystal as it was about to tumble to the floor.

His grip around her hand lingered as their gazes locked. Connor's blue eyes could charm the wings off a plane.

In another time and place, she would pursue this man. This wasn't the time or the place.

She slipped her fingers away from his.

"I should go," she said.

"You haven't heard me out."

His claim that she had a magical gift wasn't the whole story? Okay, mister knight of the round table.

"You've got five minutes and I'm out of here," she said.

"Brianna, Crealde is invisible."

CHAPTER NINE

"That does it. I'm out." Brianna stood to leave. Connor *was* imbalanced. No telling what was coming out of his mouth next.

"Wait. I'm serious," he said.

"You saw that cat. He was right here on the table."

"Only people with unique gifts can see him, Brianna."

Gifts. Gifts. Gifts. Why does he keep harping on that?

"And don't forget the pendulum," he said.

A hidden light. A magnet. There had to be some explanation.

"Echo's your grandmother, isn't she?" He asked.

Cripes. "How did you find out?"

His lips puckered to one side. "That's complicated. If I can prove Crealde is invisible will you level with me?"

Though she still thought he was missing a few screws, there wasn't much choice if she wanted this assignment to work. A story about a town full of unbalanced people would be as good as one about supernaturals posing as fake mediums and snake oil salesmen.

"Well, if you think you can prove it, sure. Why not?"

After Connor had made a few calls to arrange for the sales clerks to come in, the Carpe Diem opened for a one-night-only moonlight madness sale.

Packed from the minute the door opened, the store's check-out line never dropped below ten people for two hours. All while Crealde managed to stay put in a basket on a high shelf behind the register, in full view of anyone who made a purchase.

Connor sat on a stool nearby, smiling and visiting with customers, and offering an occasional nod to Brianna.

When a family with two small children admired a display of ceramic and stuffed cats, Brianna asked if they'd noticed how much the white ones resembled the resident store cat.

Brianna gestured to the basket then glanced at the bewildered customers whose confusion mirrored hers. Crealde was curled up in a ball, snoozing. How'd they miss that?

Back out of this and fast. "Oh, he was just there a minute ago. He must be wandering around." She pretended to look for him under the counters and around corners.

The family kept their distance from Brianna as she cast a glance at Connor. He tipped his head to the side with an 'I-told-you-so.'

She had to hand it to him for coming up with one heck of an elaborate hoax. But how did he get all these people in on it?

She needed assurance that she wasn't insane. At Crealde's basket, she reached to pet him. Her fingers disappeared into his thick, and very real, fur. His purr turned into a wide-mouth yawn.

One of the teenage clerks handed Brianna a cat treat. "Give him this and he'll be your friend for life."

Brianna shifted her eyes around the room to see if anyone was watching, then offered the treat to the cat. He sniffed it with his warm nose, then scarfed it down.

Wait just a damn minute.

That family didn't see the cat but the clerk could?

Where was the hidden camera? About now the television host should pop out from somewhere, and everyone will applaud and laugh at the good joke.

That had to be it. The whole crowd was in on this. Connor pulled off a good one. Why he'd do this, she had no idea.

Maybe these mean-spirited people were another reason her father resented Nocturne Falls.

Arms crossed over her chest, Brianna's toe tapped the floor. She'd show them. What a great hook for a story it would be to turn the tables on them.

Ten minutes went by. Then fifteen. No cameras. No production crew.

Besides herself, the only other annoyed person was a boy who stared at her as though she had three heads and horns on each, while he tried to reach something behind her.

Finally, Connor motioned for her to follow him back upstairs. She hoped her shaking legs would survive the climb.

In the kitchen, Connor poured two glasses of Merlot and offered one to Brianna.

"Believe me now?" He asked.

Brianna flicked the glass as she stared past him.

She didn't answer. He anticipated this wouldn't be easy. Coming to terms with magical gifts never was.

The discussion with his parents about being a falcon-shifter had been clumsier than their 'birds and bees' talk.

To seven-year-old Connor and eight-year-old Ryan, the concept of sprouting feathers and flying had been hysterically funny and unbelievable.

Until the night they hid behind the garage on the estate.

Unwilling to wait for their parents to make good on their promise to teach them, the brothers made their first attempt at shifting.

Trying with all their might, they had grunted and groaned as they rubbed their arms and wiggled their toes.

All while their father watched from a discrete distance. After letting them struggle, he had walked up to them and asked if they wanted to see him shift.

As ready as two boys could be, they witnessed their father change; slowly and gradually. In a matter of fact voice, he had explained what was happening to him as someone would explain how to tie knots or saw a board.

Once the shift was complete, he remained in falcon long enough to prove a point, then returned to human.

The image still etched in Connor's mind. That was the day he realized he was different. And beginning that day, their father started the process of training them to shift wisely and not on impulse.

Connor was still working on the impulse part.

Someone did a disservice to Brianna Putnam. It wasn't fair or right to let someone grow up without understanding an essential part of who they were.

Echo better know what she was doing. Connor ventured into dangerous territory.

"Brianna, if you aren't ready to talk about this, I understand."

She turned her head toward him in slow motion. "Maybe you understand. I sure don't."

The knot in her stomach grew to the size of a basketball. "Everything that happened downstairs was real, wasn't it?"

Connor nodded. "Remember when we met in the driveway? You saw Crealde. Downstairs the tourists didn't see him. But you did."

Brianna shook her head. "No. I can't believe you." It was all nonsense. "But the clerks saw him."

"Yes. And so did I. And everyone that I introduced you to in this town can see him."

The wine soured on her tongue. "May I have some water?"

Connor handed her a bottle of Moonbow water from the fridge. The cool liquid soothed her dry mouth and frazzled nerves.

"Remember when I gave you a bottle of this before?" He asked.

"I loved it. It reminded me of Oregon."

"It's bottled here especially for our tourists. We must be careful not to reveal who we are. Moonbow ensures outsiders won't be freaked out by an occasional slip-up."

She held the bottle at arm's distance, then put it down. Was the water laced with drugs?

"Why are you telling me all this?" She asked.

"Because you're Echo's granddaughter."

Why did he keep saying that? She'd told no one.

Brianna twisted her silver bracelet around her wrist until the skin turned red, then took it off and spun it so fast on the table that it flew into Connor's lap.

'This thing's solid silver.'

"Yes, it is. I've had it since I was a kid," she said.

'Probably about the time the psychic gift emerged.'

"Stop with the gift talk, Connor. I don't believe in it."

"Brianna, I never said a word."

CHAPTER TEN

"Yes, you did. You said it was solid silver."

Connor shook his head and handed the bracelet back to Brianna. "Those were my thoughts. I never said anything out loud. Your grandmother is clairsentient. She hears what people are thinking. The only way she can block it is when she's wearing a bracelet. Just like you."

Brianna extended her wrists and stared at them. In a barely audible voice, she asked, "Are you telling me the truth?"

"Nobody, even regular humans in Nocturne Falls lie about these things. Especially people like us."

Like *us*? Now what was he trying to tell her?

She slipped the bracelet back on and collected the few wits she had left. Without the bracelet, relentless voices and headaches.

With it on, her mind quieted.

"If my grandmother has some clairsentient thing going on, and maybe, just maybe, I do too, are you saying this whole town is like that place in Florida where all the mediums are supposed to live?"

Connor chuckled. "You mean Cassadega? We have a lot more than psychics here. But to answer your question, there are a few."

Oh, hallelujah. Finally, what Brianna had been waiting for. Someone to spill the beans. There had to be some scam aspect to all this.

Most psychics were tricksters. This so-called gift was just her imagination working overtime.

As she sat forward in her chair waiting to hear more, one of the clerks called upstairs for Connor to lock the doors. While he was gone, Brianna took a quick walk through the apartment.

No one had mentioned when Echo was coming home. Brianna hoped it would be before she returned to LA.

Whoever decorated this place had a passion for pink, and Brianna had to admit it grew on her. There was a sense of order among this chintzy chaos just as there was downstairs, though it was a little cramped. And lace covered. And over the top girly.

Brianna laughed as she ran her fingers over a crocheted doily on the back of an upholstered chair. She remembered that Crealde, the so-called invisible cat, wasn't a lace fan either.

How had Brianna's father managed to live here with his mother and sister? It wasn't exactly a boy's world.

"Want to see the rest of the place?"

Brianna jumped at the sound of Connor's voice over her shoulder. "I shouldn't be poking around."

"Why not? It's your grandma's home, so as much yours as hers. I'm sure she wouldn't mind."

"Where is she, anyway? Nobody will tell me."

Connor's cheeks turned crimson. Odd reaction to a simple question.

"She's on an extended trip." He shoved his hands into his pockets. "She loves traveling."

Reasonable answer. But somehow it didn't feel like the full truth.

"It's getting late and I should be leaving." At the top of the stairway she stopped. "Maybe one more favor. Could I see the bedrooms? I'm sure one of them was my father's. I doubt it looks the same."

"I'm staying in that room. I'll show you."

Brianna had followed him down a long hallway before it hit her. Though she was half-peeved at him for screwing with her mind, she was following this attractive man to his bedroom.

Cripes.

At the end of the hall, Connor flipped on the bedroom light. "Sorry for the mess. I wasn't expecting company." He threw a blanket over his unmade bed and kicked shoes and socks to the corner.

Brianna stepped through the threshold and

realized she'd walked into a time warp. Shelves were crammed with toys and books. A ball bat and glove hung on a wall. Sports trophies. Photos. High school diploma.

And not a stitch or scrap of pink anywhere.

She picked up a stuffed teddy bear from a shelf. It was missing its nose and had mended ears. She hugged the well-worn toy to her chest and nuzzled its head.

Her father never talked about living in this bubble-gum house, or in this room. What horrible thing had come between a mother and son to drive him away for so long?

Her grandmother hadn't touched anything in here. It was probably just as her son left it.

Brianna realized that she was holding her breath and that these walls were closing in on her.

"Connor, I need to get out of here." She spun toward the door. "I'm sorry. This room is creeping me out."

"Brianna, wait." Connor gently grasped her arm. "I'll walk with you."

THE FALCON TAMES THE PSYCHIC

She wiggled loose. "I'll be okay. It's not far."

Downstairs, Brianna leaned on the porch rail filling her lungs with fresh air. The boy who'd lived in that bedroom had an ordinary life. Sports. Toys. Awards. Nothing about the room felt angry or resentful.

Something deep inside her wanted to find that little boy in the tattered photo and hug him tight. And give him a safe space to explain why he grew up hating this place.

Brianna eyed the porch swing. "I need a minute." She scooted into the corner of the swing.

"May I sit with you?" Connor gestured to the spot next to her.

She really wasn't ready to go back to the Inn and could use some company.

The gentle motion of Connor's strong legs rocking the swing calmed her. No use hiding who she was any longer. Connor knew it anyway.

"My grandmother can really read minds?"

"Echo is scary good at it. She gives card readings, too."

Brianna's father banned card games. Or Ouija. Or anything else he considered dark magic. She had to sneak her Harry Potter books into the house. Though she hid them, she'd read them cover to cover, fantasizing that she lived in such a wonderful world.

"Tell me about her bracelet," she said.

"I wish Jess was here. She'd tell you everything. All I know is that when Echo takes it off, she hears the other person's thoughts as though they were talking out loud."

Hears thoughts like talking? Like those scrambled words that came into her head?

The doctors had called it everything from having secret friends that she'd grow out of, to dissociative disorder and borderline schizophrenic.

When the silver bracelet arrived, everything changed.

Her thoughts congealed like a bowl of sticky noodles. Memories of probes, adhesive patches, scans, interviews, clinics.

An invisible cat. Her father's childhood

bedroom. Finding his photo.

Everything ping ponged inside her skull.

Top it off with rocking next to a gorgeous man whose muscular thigh was centimeters from hers.

And a freaking La Grande Bouche deadline.

From the woods, a lonely animal's howl crackled the hair on the back of her neck. What next? Werewolves?

Her brilliant idea to walk alone dissolved.

"I changed my mind. I'd appreciate an escort," she said.

Somewhere between the first block past the Carpe Diem and the last block to the Inn, Connor's hand had slipped under her elbow.

He leaned close and spoke in her ear. "See the Hunter moon?"

Perhaps it was his warm breath and deep voice thrumming in her ear. Or the autumn evening dancing with the seductive wisps of his cologne that set her heart on fire.

If she could bottle this moment, she'd make a killing.

The street lamp illuminated his chiseled chin and cheekbones while he kept his eye on the sky, as though he was looking for something or someone.

Standing next to this mysterious and hot-looking man tore Brianna in half. She'd come to Nocturne Falls to write the breakthrough story.

Now it seemed she was part of it.

How would she ever make sense of what happened tonight?

Connor's grip on her elbow tightened.

"Brianna, I'd like to see you again." He cleared his throat. "I mean, to show you around. You haven't seen the falls. I'd love to show you Harmswood Academy where I went to school."

"I'd like that."

Connor took her hands in his. Before she finished a breath, he bent down and gave her a quick kiss on the lips.

Quick? Not on his life.

Brianna stood on her tiptoes and interlaced her fingers around his neck, staring into his eyes for any reason to stop.

THE FALCON TAMES THE PSYCHIC

Their second kiss was deep and tender. His lips demanded, and she answered with urgency, surprised at the desire welling from inside. The borders between their bodies disappeared as she entered a mystical, warm place.

His fingers massaged her lower back as he brought her closer, causing her tiny moan to escape into his mouth.

His rum scented aftershave and musky male scent overpowered her senses and sent tingles up her spine.

She brought her hands to his shoulders and eased away from him.

"Now, that's more like it," she said.

CHAPTER ELEVEN

Crealde the invisible.

No.

Now you see him; now you don't.

Absurd.

The fantastic, stupendous, outrageous feline.

Dumb. Dumb. And dumber.

At a small outside table at the Hallowed Bean, Brianna deleted each one.

Disgusted, she slammed the laptop shut.

She had to make something work.

After last night's delicious good night kiss with Connor, she'd made the mistake of opening an email from her editor. Her assignment ended if she didn't submit the first thousand words by five o'clock today.

Missing that deadline meant leaving Nocturne Falls and going back to the cubicle.

She and Connor had agreed to meet at 10:30, but she'd arrived an hour early to bang out ideas on her laptop. She'd wanted this done and out of her hair.

How hard was this writing thing? Staff writers turned in articles by the boatload on short notice. Why couldn't she even find the first sentence?

Connor needed a break from the frou-frou apartment. After feeding Crealde, he drove to the estate to get fresh clothes. On the outside chance he'd dodge his mother, he ducked inside through the pantry door intending to take the back stairs to his bedroom.

He tapped his finger on his lips as he passed Sabrina, the housekeeper, in the kitchen. With an eye roll toward the dining room door, Sabrina flashed three fingers, part of the secret code they'd invented to identify Solange Ford's whereabouts. His mother was in her office. Once holed up in there, she often didn't emerge for hours.

Sneaking into this McMansion required teamwork. Sabrina was the best.

With luck, he should make it upstairs without an encounter.

Taking the stairs two at a time, avoiding the squeaky boards, he reached his room where he changed into fresh khakis and a T-shirt.

House sitting had its upside. The apartment was all his. And except for Echo Stargazer's surprise visit, nobody cared if he wore clothes or not.

Back in the kitchen, he blew a kiss to Sabrina and went out the door. He'd driven Echo's truck to the house but left it parked on the street. Engine racket in the driveway would bring Solange to the door in a heartbeat.

Through the garage's glass window, he glanced at his Porsche. He hadn't driven it for three weeks. Desire to take his baby out cruising coursed through every inch of his body.

An image flashed through his mind of driving top down through the mountains. Engine purring. Gears singing praises. And Brianna Putnam beside him.

That woman's red pouty lips tasted better than he had imagined. For sure, she knew how to kiss a man.

If Echo was right, and she usually was, Brianna was up to something.

That kiss didn't mean commitment.

If she weren't so damned cute, it would be a lot easier to keep his distance. What was it about this woman that dug under his skin?

"Connor."

The flat, dispassionate announcement came from none other than Solange Ford.

"Oh, hey, Mother." As though she'd believe his nonchalant escape. So close to freedom, yet so far.

"You might show the consideration to see me before you left," Solange said.

"I thought you were busy in your office," he

said.

"I swear. Your collusions with Sabrina are comical."

Connor's spine shot stiff as rebar.

"Come on, son. Give me credit. I know when my boys are around. I need to talk to you."

Connor checked the time on his phone. He was supposed to meet Brianna in less than an hour.

"I really don't have time."

"May I surmise your hurry is about a young lady?"

"Mother, can we talk about this later?"

"In fact, we *will* talk later. I've been in touch with our few allies left on the board of directors. If we don't act by the end of the month, that special session goes forward. We don't have a majority vote, even with our additional proxies. You must go to Atlanta in person."

Part of him wanted to turn his back on this corporate BS. Yet this might be a chance to prove himself.

But his knowledge about the workings of FFG

wasn't deep enough to stand toe-to-toe with the big guns, despite intensive tutoring by his late father.

"I'd look like a fool in front of that board," he said.

"With that attitude, you most certainly would. I could coach you, but we'd need to start immediately."

"I made plans."

"Later this evening then. I understand you need to stay the night in that trashy emporium but come back for a few hours this evening and I think I can get you up to speed. Then you'll arrive in Atlanta better prepared."

"I didn't agree to this. Don't make it sound like a done deal."

"You don't seem to understand. We aren't talking about a done *deal*. Our failure to hold on to FFG means we are *done*, period."

Connor walked into the Hallowed Bean courtyard and waved at Brianna who was seated at a back table. Even in this crowd, it was easy to spot the curly haired blonde.

Her broad smile gave him hope that she wasn't angry about last night.

"Sorry I was late. Business." He pulled an empty metal chair across the bricks to her table and immediately regretted not lifting it. Though the mortals ignored the bone rattling sound, every supernatural around them slapped their hands over their ears.

Just as Brianna did.

And still she didn't believe who she was?

"Can I get you something?" He asked.

She shook her head and pointed to two empty cups.

"I need coffee," he said. Too bad they didn't serve it with Irish cream.

When he returned to the courtyard he saw that Brianna was in a heated phone call. He stood back to allow her privacy.

Though she tried to cover her mouth, his sensitive falcon ears picked up her every word.

THE FALCON TAMES THE PSYCHIC

"I don't have enough to write a whole story. I'll get your thousand words by tonight. The full story will take more time." After a period of silence, she added, "You'll get your damn exposé."

Exposé on what? Nocturne Falls? Was she cold enough to use her family connection and humiliate everyone just to promote herself?

So, this is what Echo meant about Brianna.

How close he'd come to being suckered into this little two-faced monkey's scheme.

That was about to end.

Wearing shorts on wrought iron chairs was a big mistake.

The inevitable waffle-butt might show less if Brianna shifted to adjust her position.

Or she could ignore it and hope everyone else did, too.

Or she could sit here all day.

Connor walked up next to her. "How about a ride to the falls this morning, unless you have something else going on?"

"I'd like that." She slung her computer bag over her shoulder, hiking it around to cover what she could of her back side. "I read a little about it yesterday."

Connor didn't say much on the drive to the falls. She gave up trying to pull conversation from him, though she had many questions about last night.

If anyone should be quiet, it should be her.

As it was, her brain barely comprehended what had happened.

Though it was comforting that a quirk in her genetic pool and not a psychiatric condition caused her episodes, it was more confounding why her father didn't know it. And if he did, why would he traipse her around to doctor after doctor?

She looked away from the woods outside her passenger window and back at Connor, square jawed and intently staring ahead.

She'd kissed some odd dudes in her life, but never one who claimed to be supernatural.

THE FALCON TAMES THE PSYCHIC

He looked like a living, breathing human, and certainly kissed like one.

Shivers cascaded through her.

If not human, exactly what *was* he?

CHAPTER TWELVE

"I know a short cut," Connor said.

Brianna pointed to a paved walkway. "Everyone else is over there."

"This way avoids the tourists."

She shrugged and followed him toward a narrow opening in a stand of pines and oaks.

The deeper into the woods, the cooler and more beautiful it was, yet this was certainly not a public access path.

She stepped over thick tree roots and around rocks, nearly slipping twice trying to match Connor's long stride.

He marched up the path like a man on a

mission, glancing back only once.

Something was different about him this morning, and she wasn't sure she liked it.

What had happened to change him into this cold fish?

Connor's pace picked up when they came to a smooth plateau.

She stopped to catch her breath. "Would you slow down a little? I can't keep up."

He kept going. "Only a little farther."

What was Mister Personality's problem? Couldn't he at least give her the courtesy of looking over his shoulder?

His 'little farther' took new meaning as she stood at the base of a sharp rise at least ten feet high. Thinking for sure he'd help her up, Brianna fumed as she watched Connor's backside disappear over the ridge.

She hadn't dressed for mountain climbing and had no interest in scaling this rock pile.

But she wasn't about to let him get the best of her, either.

Looking up to the top, she shielded the sun from her eyes with one hand as she batted away gnats.

If he'd climbed it, she could too. Too bad Connor's stride was twice hers.

She plotted a path and where she'd put each foot along the way. The first two steps were easy and the pitch wasn't that steep. She'd do this. No problem.

She'd show Connor, wherever he was. At least no one was following her and snapping photos. She was certain her backside was not in a flattering pose. What excellent fodder for her friends to plaster over social media.

It wasn't long until the gradual incline turned nasty. She struggled to get a foothold on the mossy stones, slipping once and smacking her ankle on a rock.

Say hello to some serious pain.

She grabbed at a branch to steady her footing.

While she wobbled on uncertain ground, Brianna's anger boiled.

THE FALCON TAMES THE PSYCHIC

She'd had about all she could take of this short-cut stuff. Why hadn't he followed everyone else up the nice paved path?

Was he trying to prove something?

Or leave her in the woods to die?

That was stupid. What would he gain from that, especially after going to all the trouble of the big reveal last night?

Once on even ground, her resolve married fury. She stomped her way toward where the path took a sharp right turn.

If Connor Ford thought this was funny, it wasn't. And she would tell him about it, once she found him.

Leaves rustled in a branch above her and she jumped. What was she expecting? A werewolf? Bigfoot?

"Don't even think about it, who or whatever you are." She glanced up but saw nothing. "Go about your business."

The branches moved as something flew away.

"This is getting ridiculous."

She charged forward to the bend in the path that opened to bright sunlight. In a clearing, sitting on a large stone and leaning against a tree, Connor.

"Took you long enough," he said.

Brianna's teeth clamped hard enough that they might crack. "I was enjoying the lovely scenery and the wildlife. Such a charming nature walk."

He flashed the first real smile she'd seen on him all morning.

"See anything interesting?" He asked.

"Let's see. I fought off a couple of pterodactyls." She dusted leaf litter off her bare knees. "But that only took a minute or two."

Connor choked on his barrel laugh.

At least he still had an ounce of humor in him.

She spotted a small feather, picked it up, and held it to the sunlight. Slate gray, brown and white colors blended as though painted by an artist.

"Is this from a hawk?" She asked.

"Falcon."

"Ever seen one around here?"

He shot her a cryptic smile. "A few."

THE FALCON TAMES THE PSYCHIC

She tucked the feather behind her ear and stood in front of him, her hands on her hips. "So, what was the idea of leaving me alone to struggle? I could have used a little help."

"You made it, didn't you?"

Oooh. He'd plucked her last nerve with that.

"Look, I don't know what I did to torque you off, but if you plan to be a jerk the whole time, take me back to town."

"You're missing the point." His voice was so strange.

Brianna teetered on the verge of a meltdown as she vice gripped the flesh above her hips. "And what *is* the point?"

"The falls. You won't see much if you keep standing with your back to it."

Brianna sliced her gaze up, then to each side. She slid her hands behind her back where she threaded her fingers in a knot.

Glancing down, she made a slow turn. A waterfall is a waterfall. She doubted this would be anything special. She'd grown up a few miles from the Columbia River where waterfalls were—

"Gorgeous," she whispered. All her bitterness and anger melted at the sight of this magnificent falls. "It's enchanting. I feel good all over just looking at it."

"Now see why so many people come here?"

"And Moonbow water?"

"From nearby falls. There are several around here but this is the main one."

His tone and attitude had improved a hundred percent. Perhaps this *was* a magical place, if she believed in that stuff. Something had affected him and for the better.

Standing at her side, he pointed out places around the falls where he and his brother had played as little kids.

Were these Fords part goat? That would explain how easy it would be for little boys to scale rocks. But it didn't make for a sexy visual nor did the thought that she kissed a smelly goat.

Connor placed his hand lightly on her lower back and pointed. "See that small stand of trees over there? Those pines were our lookout where we watched the tourists."

She had no idea where he pointed. All the trees looked alike to her.

"Follow my finger." He traced a line in the air in front of her, then up an angle, then stopped. "There's a stand of pine trees taller than the others around them."

If what she saw was the place, it was at least a quarter mile away and on the far side of the falls. How did he expect her to see that far?

"I'll take your word for it," she said.

From the corner of her eye, Brianna caught a hint of a blush blooming across his cheeks.

Even with all his moodiness today, Connor exuded sexy and she couldn't believe she was standing here with him. And not back in her room where she should be hammering out a story.

Her feelings for him weren't helping her growing guilt-trip. If. No. *When* she filed this story, she'd get out of town and never look back.

She stepped away, took her phone from her

347

pocket, and took photos. "I'm glad you talked me into—"

Her words and her feet splayed in opposite directions as Connor grabbed her waist.

"Almost one step too far." His resonating voice and breath in her ear worsened control of her scrambling feet and her heart.

At a safe distance from the edge, Connor held on to her until she regained her balance.

"That might have been ugly," he said, his arms still around her.

"Yes, but what a terrific headline. Woman gets world record freefall selfie." She turned to see his reaction to the lame joke, but her heart plummeted at the look on his face.

"You're white as a ghost," she said.

"Brianna, it isn't funny. Every year out of towners do some pretty stupid stuff around here and pay for it."

"But nothing happened, Connor." She opened her arms out to her sides. "See, I'm fine."

When he didn't say anything, and kept staring

at her, all she thought about were the times she accounted to her father for some dumb thing that had gone wrong. He'd go silent right before he'd launch into a yelling fit.

She and her brother learned early to cover for each other so they wouldn't catch the man's grief, at least not as often.

Connor didn't seem the type to go ballistic, but she'd only known him a short time. What was going on with him? Why didn't he say something?

"Connor?"

He stepped closer and in a blink, took her into his arms.

Swift and quick, his kiss paralyzed her.

This one wasn't like the other night. Not curious. Not cute.

This one was all-out hunger. His hands moved to the nape of her neck then into her hair, where his fingers made gentle circles on her scalp, finding the places that always sparked an electrical explosion. Half the thunder bolt left through her toes. The other half through the top of her head.

Her hands skimmed his back until they stopped on his arms where she remembered those tattoos. His wings. Enfolding her. Protecting her.

He released Brianna's lips, then nibbled down her neck.

An electrical buzz ran the circuit over her body.

She wanted his lips on hers again, but she didn't want him to stop what he was doing.

Connor whispered something that she didn't quite understand. Then he caressed her breast.

It had to stop. Now before it was too late. She stepped back, panting.

She would not tangle her emotions any worse than they already were. Once she left town, she didn't want any regrets, or even more, guilt.

"Don't get me wrong. I like you a lot. But you know as well as me that nothing could come of this," she said.

"Because of the story?"

Brianna's spine steeled at the same time her breathing halted.

Connor picked up a small rock and rolled it

between his fingers. "I heard you on the phone talking to someone about a story. About Nocturne Falls."

He threw the stone in the direction of the falls. It fell far short of its mark and dropped into the deep woods.

CHAPTER THIRTEEN

"This town has survived a lot worse threats than you." He looked away from Brianna. "For your sake, I hope whatever they're paying is worth it."

That's what's wrong. Connor had overheard her on the phone this morning with her editor.

Brianna had spoken out of spite and frustration. Now she knew there was no story here and certainly not one about a haven of lunatics.

She was over carrying her father's bitterness on her shoulders.

Too many things swirled in her mind. One, coming to terms with a so-called psychic gift. Two, her feelings for this mysterious Connor Ford.

Three, climbing down the trail without breaking her neck.

"You knew all this and still brought me up here? I'll let the part about leaving me with the dinosaurs go, for now. If you think I'm the evil one, why'd you kiss me?" She asked.

"The truth? I'm not sure why."

"Because you liked it?" And she hoped it signaled his feelings for her.

"Maybe. Or a goodbye kiss."

After a silent ride, Connor dropped Brianna off at the Inn. Skipping supper and a shower, she huddled under the bedcovers and sobbed into her pillow.

Connor's words clanged like a cathedral bell. *'Survived worse than you.'*

As though she'd become a plague.

She hadn't come here with the intention of falling in love with the town. Or with Connor Ford.

What the hell was she going to do now?

The magenta sunset splashed across the sky was lost on Connor. Parked in the Carpe Diem driveway, he stared a hole through the truck's dashboard.

No woman ever had gotten under his skin like Brianna. The plan to let her stumble up the path to scare her a little, and give her a lesson about messing with his town and his friends, blew up in his face.

He'd assumed she would give up halfway, tuck her tail, and yell for help. All fine except she didn't need help. When she didn't cry out, he'd shifted to falcon, and risked her seeing him, to be sure she was okay.

Though he never pictured her as the rock climbing type, Brianna had scrambled to the top by herself. When she broke through to the clearing, and the sun glinted off her golden curls, it took mammoth restraint not to grab her into his arms right then.

Her stubborn resilience to hang on and keep climbing had amazed him.

THE FALCON TAMES THE PSYCHIC

At the same time, it served as a warning that she wouldn't give up easy on this story idea, even if it meant selling out her grandmother's town.

And why had he kissed her again?

To break her down and get the truth?

Kissing her was a big, wonderful mistake. If he hadn't acted on his desire to hold her in his arms, she'd be packed and gone by now. And he wasn't ready for that.

He opened then slammed shut the truck's door.

"Oh, hell." He'd forgotten about the meeting with his mother.

What a wonderful way to cap off the evening.

Profit and loss. Quarterly earnings. Fund performance indicators.

Not exactly the topics Connor wanted to discuss two hours after holding the foxy little Brianna Putnam in his arms.

But if that's what Solange wanted, she'd get it. He didn't hold back a nickel's worth.

An hour later, Solange leaned forward.

"Well. I had no idea you were this versed in finance. Or that you knew anything about our company."

Perhaps his father's lessons had drilled into Connor better than he thought. He'd held his own with his mother.

Connor controlled the urge to gloat. "Latent genius, I guess." And his secret love of reading business news journals.

His mother's grin cut across her face. "The most important thing is to exude confidence a shade lighter than cocky. Come into that room like you own it, and them. In fact, you do. If they sense weakness they'll go at your throat like tigers on an antelope."

"Lovely analogy."

"Truth, son. I've seen them. But I also observed your father in charge of that crowd. He was magnificent. No one in the room intimidated that man. Somehow it seems you're channeling your father. And I couldn't be happier."

THE FALCON TAMES THE PSYCHIC

And Connor couldn't be more exhausted.

He rolled into the Carpe Diem driveway at eleven forty-five. As he climbed the stairs to the apartment, dread poured over him.

Crealde.

He hadn't fed the cat since this morning.

Connor prepared for every possible worst case scenario.

Would the theatrical feline be on his back, playing out a Shakespearean death?

Would he aim a tiny sawed off shotgun at the door, ready to shoot the first person who walked inside?

Or maybe as soon as he opened the door he'd be arrested by an animal rescue swat team.

What had Solange said? Enter the room with confidence a shade lighter than cocky.

Connor breezed into the kitchen and flipped on the light.

"Okay, buddy. Ready for a midnight snack? How do we get to *yes* on this?"

A tin of flaked tuna fired across the floor,

careened off Connor's foot, rebounded under the kitchen table, and stopped short of the cat's food dish.

Connor expected that swat team any minute.

"But there isn't any story." Brianna put the phone on speaker and tossed it on her bed. "I was wrong, Angus." About everything.

"I don't give a damn if you think you were wrong. You hounded me for weeks about that town. Fakes and scammers. Crooks. Thieves. That's all you talked about so I funded your trip to Georgia. This morning you told me, and I'm quoting, 'You'll get your damn story.'"

"Angus, but—"

"But, *hell.* I want a story, or you're fired. Got it?" The man's guttural snorts thundered through the phone like a raging bull about to charge.

Long after the call ended, Brianna sat in a chair across the room, hugging her knees to her chest. She stared at the phone still in the same spot on the bed.

What was she afraid of? That Angus-the-bogeyman would ooze out of it and chase her like a banshee around the room?

Or that she knew her decision? That's what frightened her more.

The only way to write this 'damn story' was to make it up. She hadn't read or seen anything that remotely resembled black magic or carnival charades.

With one exception. Crealde. And her ability to see him.

That was a large exception.

She had to try her hand at a draft. It would be pure fiction, but at least something on paper.

This would give her time to calm down and reconcile her feelings. If Angus fired her, so be it. She'd go home for a while and sort things out.

If she sent the story and by some miracle it published, she'd embarrass a whole town and especially Connor Ford.

Either way, story or not, staying in Nocturne

Falls was out of the question. With one foot in the natural world and the other somewhere, she didn't quite know where, she didn't belong here. Or deserve to be here.

Brianna opened her laptop. Once she started, the words tumbled out on the page. By two-thirty in the morning, she'd finished five-thousand words, enough for at least two articles in Angus's tabloid rag.

Full of poppycock and drivel, it was a middle-of-the-night, hastily written crock of junk about every person she'd met in town. Total fabrication and the stuff of fairy tales. Just the thing for La Grande Bouche.

She'd changed the names of the townsfolk, but she'd assigned each one a fantastic character.

The flower shop owner was a reincarnated 17th-century European fairy princess. The concrete gargoyle was a frog waiting for the princess's kiss.

The sheriff was a wizard.

Connor was an avenger of evil.

That would teach Angus a good lesson about

ultimatums.

Brianna had a gut feeling it was going to be a long winter hanging out in Portland coffee shops, sipping espresso, and scouring online job sites. Time to dig out the wool sweaters from storage, unless her mother had already donated them.

Brianna reread the story.

Though it was off-the-wall absurd, it was pretty good. Might make a nice novella someday.

But nobody in their right mind would believe a word of it.

CHAPTER FOURTEEN

"My cousin? Here? In Nocturne Falls?" Jess Callahan's carry-on bag landed on the floor with a loud thud that drove Crealde from under the table and into a back bedroom. "Could you have given me a heads-up?"

"I wasn't sure how to tell you. I didn't know it was your cousin until your grandmother told me." Connor dropped his chin. That wasn't exactly the best way to lead into this discussion. Oh well, the cat was out now; literally.

"My grandmother? Nana? What are you talking about?"

"What's going on?" Ryan Ford came through

the kitchen door hefting two more suitcases. "I heard Jess all the way downstairs."

"You should unpack first then we'll talk," Connor said.

"No. We'll talk first." Jess took a seat at the dining room table. "Our flight from Boston to Atlanta was hell on wings. The bags came in on the next flight. Ryan's car battery had died in long-term parking. My headache's splitting."

She crossed her arms over her chest and wiggled into position like a hen on a nest.

"Maybe later?" Connor asked.

"I'm all ears," she said. "Now, please."

For the next half hour Connor did his best to run the narrative, though the retelling was lame as a one-legged goose.

Jess remained silent through the entire recitation. Ryan interjected with a few questions.

And Connor, who had run out of steam, opened his palms to the ceiling. "That's all I got. She's staying at the Gingerbread Inn."

Jess slowly nodded. "I'm going to unpack and

take a hot shower," she said through tightly pursed lips.

Once they heard the water running, Connor felt it was safe to talk to his brother.

"I've never seen her this upset," he said.

"She's just venting. That family has a lot of drama," Ryan said.

"Doesn't ours?"

Ryan ignored the comment and continued. "After Jess's parents died, her uncle refused to take her in. That's how she ended up with Echo."

Connor snapped to attention. "Refused? Why?"

"She's never told me. I'm not sure she even understands. I think she met her cousins once but a long time ago when they were kids. Does the woman look anything like Jess?"

"Not one bit. She's short. Curly blonde hair. Huge blue eyes. Curves in the right places." He trailed off, remembering what it was like to hold her. Their soft kiss. Her flowery perfume.

The bewildered look in her eyes when she tried to chew him out for letting her climb the rocks alone.

"She's got a lot of sass and style," Connor said.

"Bro, this sounds like—".

"Don't say it. Just don't."

Sweat poured like overflowing creeks down Connor's shirt. This would either be ingenious, or an epic fail.

Ryan had spent two days calming down Jess; the same amount of time Connor needed to talk Brianna into seeing him again and meeting her cousin.

Both brothers walked on eggshells as they fired up the barbecue grill.

"It would save our bacon if Echo would show up tonight," Ryan said.

"Don't count on it," Connor said. Though she'd be mighty welcome.

The screen door slammed and Connor glanced up at Jess balancing a foil-wrapped platter as she came down the wooden stairs.

"My cousin's the one I'd bet won't show." Jess handed Connor the platter of chicken and a jumbo Portobello mushroom for the vegan, Ryan.

"She'll be here." Connor had offered to pick up Brianna, but she'd been adamant that she'd come alone.

Jess shrugged as she hooked her hand around Ryan's arm.

Jess and Ryan. An unlikely pair but completely suited for each other. Yin to the other's yang. The stuff in sappy movies. Still, they brought the best out in each other.

Connor only hoped that one day the right woman would drop into his life.

"Is this her?" Ryan whispered.

Connor took a deep breath and turned. Oh, yes it was.

Brianna walked toward them, wearing the same killer red dress she'd worn the first day he'd met her. His heart rate skyrocketed. He licked his parched lips and tried to speak.

The only sound that emerged was a lame

crackle.

Ryan handed his brother a bottle of water and stepped forward toward their guest.

"Brianna?" Ryan offered his hand. "I'm Ryan. It's a pleasure to meet you." He gestured to Jess, standing at a distance behind him. "Your cousin."

Jess didn't move. Her expression was stone sober. This was not good.

Brianna must be freaking. Connor stepped to her side and lightly touched her lower back. The smell of her perfume was intoxicating. She leaned closer so their bodies touched.

"Are you two women going to stand there in a stare down all evening?" Connor asked.

"It's been a very long time," Brianna said.

Jess nodded. "It's good to see you."

Connor thought he felt a small quake in Brianna's touch.

"Anyone care for a drink?" Ryan asked.

"Beer." The women's simultaneous answer caused both to laugh, if only a small one, and only for a fraction of a second.

Connor took that as a positive sign as he retrieved two bottles from a cooler.

Ryan and Connor attempted to drag conversation from the cousins through dinner but failed at every turn.

With nothing left to lose, and his tolerance for this standoff exasperated, Connor decided it was time to cut this mess to the chase.

"Brianna, I told Ryan and Jess why you're in Nocturne Falls. And I told them you can see Crealde."

Brianna toyed with her food. "I figured you would."

"Did he also tell you these gifts run in our family? I'm clairvoyant. Nana, our grandmother, is clairsentient," Jess said.

Brianna kept her head bowed. "Yes, he told me."

"It's nothing to be ashamed about. A natural part of our lives, though it took me a few years to get used to it," Jess said.

"They told me I was crazy." Brianna turned the

silver bracelet around her wrist.

"Who told you that?" Jess asked.

"Everyone." Brianna looked at her beautiful red-haired cousin, her face shrouded in confusion. This meeting must be hard on her, too.

"But I'm not crazy." Brianna's voice barely rose above a whisper. "I'm not."

Ryan sniffed a laugh and hugged Jess. "If you are, then we all are."

"If we don't block our vibes they will drive you nuts." Jess held up her right hand. "This jade ring blocks my visions. I can't predict what I'll see when I take it off. So, I don't."

"When did they start?" Brianna asked.

"After I moved here. You know my parents died, right?"

Brianna gave a slight nod. "I was very little. I remember my parents talking about somebody dying. I didn't understand who."

Jess continued. "This was my mother's ring. She was clairvoyant like me. This ring kept her sane and blocked the visions. After she died, Nana gave it to me when I was about eight. That's when I started to see things."

"Eight? That's when my nightmares started. And then the voices. And when grandmother sent this bracelet to me."

"That's the one you left at the bar," Connor said.

"Why did I take it off in the first place? Nerves, I guess. I had bad dreams all that night. I barely slept. Then I had a horrible headache the next morning until I found it."

"Nana blocks with a bracelet, too." Jess fixed her eyes on Brianna. "I see a lot of Nana in you. You're about the same height and body type."

"Where is she, anyway?" Brianna asked.

Connor, Ryan, and Jess scanned the four corners of the room.

Brianna followed with her eyes.

"We aren't a hundred percent sure," Jess said.

Brianna shook her head. "What's that mean?"

"It's a long story. We'll explain later," Connor said.

THE FALCON TAMES THE PSYCHIC

Tension hovered over the dinner table like filmy gauze, though it dissipated somewhat, thanks to the brothers' efforts to keep to light topics.

To Brianna, it seemed these people had an agenda and were waiting to pounce on her with it.

But what and why? Jess Callahan was a beautiful, happy woman. Far from what Brianna had imagined.

Jess and Brianna's brother, Samuel, were both tall with that red hair, just like Brianna's father. Hadn't Jess said Brianna looked like Echo?

And Ryan and Jess seemed like the perfect couple. Comfortable and loving together. It was obvious they genuinely liked each other.

When she could, and not be too obvious, Brianna exchanged smiles with Connor.

He'd worked hard to arrange this meeting. She had to hand it to him for taking the chance so she'd meet at least one of her relatives.

After coffee and dessert, they went into the

living room. Jess and Ryan sat together on a two-seat sofa.

Since Crealde filled an overstuffed chair, Brianna took the only available empty seat; a hardback armchair across from them. Connor sat on the floor, half-way between Brianna and the sofa.

With all three of them staring at her, the only thing missing to make this a real interrogation was a bright, hot light.

"Nana taught me to understand and use the gift. I'm sorry you didn't have the same privilege," Jess said.

There it was again. Gift. Brianna would never accept this.

How could these seemingly sane people believe this stuff?

She scanned their faces. No suspicious clues.

Intent and sexy as hell, Connor's eyes riveted on hers. But he couldn't disguise the fear lurking in them.

Were they stringing her along? But why would they?

"Brianna?" Connor asked. "You're awfully quiet."

No kidding.

Brianna gripped the chair arms. Her throat tightened as she stared straight at her cousin. "Can you prove you are clairvoyant?"

CHAPTER FIFTEEN

"I don't think she has to prove anything." Ryan moved his hand from around Jess's shoulders and leaned forward.

Brianna took in a deep breath at what sounded like his warning.

Jess rested her hand on Ryan's arm. "It's okay. That's exactly what I'd ask if I were her. When I take off the ring, I have no idea what vision I'll see. I can't control it. And I don't like to tempt it. For example, I tried to see where Nana was, but that vision didn't come through."

"Last summer, Jess saw a forest fire thirty

miles away. She saved our animal sanctuary," Ryan said.

Sure. And just last week, Brianna jumped over the top of the Los Angeles City Hall.

Jess slipped off the jade ring and handed it to Ryan.

"I don't like this," Ryan said.

"Don't worry. Hand it back when I ask." Jess closed her eyes.

There wasn't a sound in the room except the ticking of a wall clock and Crealde's light snore.

As though tethered by an invisible cord, Brianna couldn't pull her eyes away from her cousin. If this was a parlor trick, the set up was brilliant.

After several minutes, Jess's eyes flashed open. "Not everything I saw makes sense."

Brianna gave Jess credit. She had the dramatic act down pat. Her cousin hadn't seen a damn thing.

"You work for La Grande Bouche," Jess said.

A simple deduction that anyone could find online. "Yes."

"I see an angry confrontation. You need to be careful, Brianna. He's not to be trusted."

"Who?"

"A man. In his fifties. Silver hair."

That gave Brianna nothing to go on. "That's pretty generic."

"His name is Angus."

There it was. The big finale just like those TV mediums.

"Connor heard me on the phone. I probably said Angus's name. A little Internet work and you put the pieces together," Brianna said.

Jess slipped her jade ring on and shook her head. "Not everyone who sees, believes."

"I'm sorry. I just don't buy it." Brianna turned her bracelet around on her wrist.

"The inscription says '*Forever in my heart*,'" Jess whispered.

"Echo told you that," Brianna snapped back. "Or Connor. I left it at the bar." Impulsively, Brianna slid the bracelet off and waved it at the trio.

"That's how the bartender identified it. You

told them didn't you, Connor?" Brianna covered her eyes to hide her tears as the bracelet slipped from her hand and rolled in front of Connor. "Why are you all lying to me?"

How she'd wanted this fairy tale to be real. She'd gone her whole life not fitting in anywhere. This seemed like such a nice little town. Then they had to pull this nonsense.

She'd held this inside for so long. Of all the worst times, in front of three strangers, tears streamed down her cheeks.

Connor came through first. 'I knew this would be too much.'

Jess next. 'Nana, it would be a good time for you to drop by.'

At the touch of Connor's hand on her shoulder, Brianna raised her head. He held the bracelet out to her. "Better put this on."

"You didn't say anything out loud, did you?" Brianna asked.

Jess shook her head as she handed her cousin a glass of water.

"Any chance you like Tai Chi?" Ryan asked.

Jess waved her hand toward Ryan. "Inside joke, Brianna. It doesn't take psychic ability to see you're in a mess. You aren't the first skeptic who wanted to out us. You won't be the last. From what I saw, you promised something to this Angus person, and now you can't produce."

Brianna stared into her glass then looked straight at Jess. "I don't know what to think. Everyone and everything about Nocturne Falls looks normal. I came here looking for a story about a bunch of whackos pretending to be monsters and bogeymen."

When the brothers bristled and flashed irritated glances, Jess put a calming hand on Ryan's arm.

"Nocturne Falls is home to many kinds of people, not just psychics. It's not easy to explain this but there are many dimensions to the universe. Some you can see easily. Some you can't," Jess said.

Where was her cousin going with this?

"With a few exceptions, for example myself,

most people living here aren't fully human," Jess said.

Brianna nearly choked. "What? I've met a lot of them. They are as human as me."

"Exactly. They have a side that appears human," Jess said.

"Don't tell me that the librarian or Sheriff Merrow, or Ian at the Poisoned Apple aren't human?"

"I'm not sure she's ready," Connor said.

"Ready for what? So, tell me about Ian," Brianna said.

"He's an elf," Jess said.

Brianna lost it. She gasped through laughter. "And I suppose Delaney Ellingham is a broom-riding witch."

"She's a vampire," Jess said.

The trio certainly knew how to play it straight. "How about the sheriff?"

"A wolf," Connor said.

The whole lot of them should be institutionalized. "Fine. I get it. And you and your brother are vampires."

"Remember, that's Delaney." Jess reached for Ryan's knee. "Connor and Ryan are falcons."

Brianna smacked her palm on her forehead. "Of course, they are. Why didn't I guess that? So, Connor, if you're a falcon why don't you just ruffle some feathers and prove it?"

"That's not how it works," Connor said.

"Because you aren't one, that's why." She bumped her glass on the chair arm and splashed water on her arm. "You're all a bunch of con artists. I've had enough for one night. Thank you for dinner, but I need to go."

She darted through the back door and down the steps into the darkness.

Connor followed. "Wait. I'll walk you back."

She held up her hand. "If I need help I'll just call the wolf. Sorry, I mean, the sheriff."

Brianna stared at her computer screen after making minor tweaks to her story, then picked up the snow globe again.

This time there was no magical water running over the falls.

She put it back on the bed stand beside the photo and the feather she'd found. Three souvenirs of the strangest place she'd ever seen.

Angus's revised story was done. Chock full of wolves, vampires, falcons, and other made up creatures, it was a whole lot better than the teaser she'd sent earlier.

"Ready or not, here you go." With an artistic flourish, Brianna spider-crawled her fingers above the keys, then hit 'submit.'

She leaned back on the bed and replayed the nonsense she'd heard tonight. They'd put a lot of work into calling her bluff.

And she'd almost bought it.

But Connor and Ryan Ford were falcon shifters?

She touched her hand to her lips.

Connor's kiss came from a very warm-blooded male. His strong arms and rock-solid chest didn't belong to a bird.

Nor did his broad shoulders that felt like velvet steel as her hands slid down his back. Nor did his strong fingers that got lost in her hair.

She picked up the feather again. Connor had insisted it was from a falcon.

Her quick online search confirmed it. And this one was from a Peregrine—the fastest animal on the planet.

Mother of oyster pearl.

That rustling in the trees above her on the trail. Had that been Connor? No possible way.

If she accepted that truth, then dominoes would fall everywhere. Ian. Delaney. Ryan. Sheriff Merrow. Everyone in every store? Restaurant? The library? The Inn proprietor?

Even Connor?

The glorious relief she'd anticipated after sending the story had U-turned into heartbreak.

What the hell had she just done?

She heard a gentle tapping on the door. Who'd knock this late?

THE FALCON TAMES THE PSYCHIC

Brianna looked through the peephole.

Connor? What did he want? How did he find her room?

She was wrapped in enough guilt as it was, let alone the mind-bender that he might be exactly what Jess Callahan said he was. A frigging falcon.

"Brianna. Please, I need to talk to you."

She leaned against the door with one hand on the knob, the other on the chain. Inside this locked room, she retreated into a cocooned reality that people were people, though some like Angus were dirt bags.

Outside that door stood Connor Ford. An attractive man that any sensible *warm-blooded* woman would latch on to in a minute.

If a woman was into falcons.

CHAPTER SIXTEEN

It would serve him right if Brianna never opened that door.

Connor wanted to kick himself for letting her walk back to the Inn alone.

He didn't fear for her safety in downtown Nocturne Falls. It was her state of mind that frightened him.

"I'll stay out here all night so either you open the door, or you'll find me asleep on the floor in the morning. Your call," he said.

After what seemed like an eternity, he heard the chain slide and the click of the handle.

Brianna opened the door a crack. "Go home,

Connor."

An Inn guest walked past with her nose turned up in disgust. Connor greeted her with a nod and a bright grin. "Sleep well," he said.

Brianna shut and relocked the door.

Connor slid to the floor, sat cross legged, leaned on the door jam, and began singing.

"Ninety-nine bottles of beer on the wall. Ninety-nine bottles of beer. Take one down, pass it around, ninety-eight bottles of beer on the wall."

When he got to the eighty-fifth bottle, Brianna opened the door, and Connor tumbled backward into the room.

"I hate that song worse than any other in the world," Brianna said as she choked back her rising giggle.

"It was a toss-up between that and the wheels on the bus go round and round."

Brianna winced. "How did you know what room I was in?"

"Friends in high places."

"And in the trees no doubt."

Connor stretched to get the kinks out of his back. "May I sit down?"

Gesturing to a chair next to the window, Brianna caught her fingers in the curtain.

"Is everything in town chintz-bombed like this place?" She muttered as she shook her fingers free from the lacy web.

"I apologize if we came on a little strong," he said.

She sat on the end of the bed as far from Connor as possible. "Oh, think nothing of it. Believe me, I've forgotten all about it."

Even snarky, she was hands down delectable. "It's a lot to take in."

She scraped her fingers through her hair and stared past him.

"You heard the part about me being a falcon, right?"

"Umm. Right."

She'd drifted far from this room.

"Brianna?"

She made a quick headshake. "Sorry. You said

something?"

"I said I'm a three-legged platypus. And I might shift any minute."

"Connor, I sent the story."

Hello. "To that Angus guy, I suppose?"

She repeatedly stabbed a pencil into a notepad on the bed stand.

"I came home so mad I could have eaten nails." The pencil lead shattered. "I can't take it back now. It's gone." She covered her face with her hands.

"How bad is it?"

Brianna pulled up a copy and let Connor read it. Half-way through he shut the laptop. He didn't need to finish. He had his answer.

If this story went public, there would be hell to pay.

"Maybe he won't believe it," Brianna said.

"I don't know about that. Gotta hand it to you. You're a good writer."

Brianna hugged a pillow to her chest. "What am I going to do? Because of me, everyone in this town will be embarrassed, or worse. I'm such a fool."

Connor moved to sit beside her. "Look, if there's a contest for the biggest fool, I'll win by a landslide. I've been in more trouble than you could ever dream up in a hundred years. And I've figured out some creative ways out of bad ones. Let me think on this and see what I come up with."

"I can't ask for your help," she whispered.

"So, don't." Connor softly touched her chin and tipped it toward him. Her round lips begged his kiss, but it would be unfair to take advantage of her now.

"I'll come by in the morning and take you to breakfast then we'll talk about the plan."

"You have one already?"

Not actually, but he would by then unless he'd lost his touch for last minute butt-savers. "Of course."

He started to leave but was stopped by Brianna's touch on his hand.

"Were you in the trees watching me while I flailed around in the dinosaur forest?"

"You weren't flailing."

She squinted her stare at him. "You could have helped me out."

"You had a great hold on that vine."

She attempted to elbow his ribs, but he gripped her arm before she inflicted a mortal wound. Their laughing eyes met, then her gaze softened.

"Would you kiss me?" She asked.

Before Brianna changed her mind, Connor pulled her into his arms and covered her mouth with his. She relaxed into his embrace and returned his kiss, finding his tongue with hers.

Probing and exploring. Melting into each other.

Maybe she was human, but she had a supernatural hold on his heart. And on this nice, soft, queen sized bed, he could claim her as his mate.

In the distance, a phone buzzed. His? Brianna's? Did it matter?

Brianna broke the kiss and found her phone. Her face blanched as she read the message.

"You are freaking kidding." Her words

rebounded off the walls. "He can't be serious."

"What? Who?"

"Angus freaking loves the story. He's coming here the day after tomorrow to see the place for himself. Now what? We have to stop him."

Connor churned his thoughts. There was a way. The hard part would be to get his family to buy-in, but with a little finesse, he'd make it happen.

"If he wants to see Nocturne Falls, then we'll show it to him," he said.

"You've never met Angus. I'm telling you this is horrible. You don't want him here. He will take the little bit I wrote and turn it into a nightmare."

Nightmare? No possible way. Angus whoever-he-was would be no match for Nocturne Falls. In fact, it might prove to be a pleasant diversion.

"Leave this to me. But promise you'll be open to anything," he said.

He hoped her quiet pause meant she was considering it. She rolled her lower lip between her teeth, then puckered into a seductive pout. Her eyes began to sparkle, and she flashed a hint of an impish grin.

"Does this plan involve creatures with wings?" She asked.

Connor's relief danced on his exhale. "Everything is in the realm of possibility. Remember, breakfast tomorrow. Meet me downstairs at eight-thirty."

He gave her a quick kiss. "Don't worry. I've got this."

CHAPTER SEVENTEEN

Nothing compared to deerskin leather.

Connor caressed the Porsche's steering wheel, then glanced into the rearview mirror to secure his ball cap.

The engine's crescendo surged through him as each system revved into a full-throated symphony.

How he'd missed this car.

With Ryan and Jess back, his house-sitting assignment ended. Good news, he had his car again. Bad news, he was back under his mother's roof and hated it.

Though he'd lived a month inside a shoebox apartment over the Carpe Diem, he came and went without anyone giving a crap. Anyone except the voracious Crealde.

And Echo Stargazer's all-to-hell embarrassing visit.

Once out on the highway, he accelerated to the speed limit plus a mile or two. No sense in pushing his luck. Or getting another speeding ticket.

He looked at his reflection in the mirror. Backward cap. T-shirt.

Music blasting from the sound system.

Lead foot on the accelerator.

If he accepted what his mother felt was his rightful seat as chairman of the board and moved to Atlanta, that would mean moving off the estate. For good.

Yeah.

Connor Ford as chairman material? But, he'd be back in Atlanta. Good times.

And Sayonara, Nocturne Falls. Though after showing Brianna around this month, he realized it wasn't that bad at all.

Ryan and Jess had decided to stay here after

their upcoming wedding in December. That would keep his mother happy to have one son close, especially if her other son was running the business.

Closer to town, the road paralleled the trail where he'd caught up with Brianna the afternoon they'd jogged back to town together.

People were already out running and biking. Cool mornings like this were ideal.

If he didn't have the breakfast date with Brianna, he'd have logged in a fast five. But thinking about her jazzed up his heart equaling a six-miler.

As beautiful as she was impetuous, Brianna was nothing like any woman he'd met. She didn't take crap from anyone. She was bright. Smart. And had a gorgeous body that fed a man's fantasy.

But misguided as hell.

If she'd admit her gift and use that energy, she'd be a dynamo. With someone like her at his side, what amazing things they could do with FFG.

All these were useless dreams that would fly to thunder once they went separate ways.

THE FALCON TAMES THE PSYCHIC

He'd come up with a plan to bail her out of this Bouche mess, and with luck and a little help, the idea might work.

But would Brianna be strong enough to go the distance with him?

Fresh croissants. Real butter. Homemade peach preserves.

Brianna scanned the tiny, handwritten signs in front of each breakfast item.

Granola. Fresh fruit. Swiss cheese and spinach quiche.

And nothing appealed.

Her appetite had tanked the minute she read Angus's email last night. She'd already arranged with the Gingerbread Inn manager for Connor to have her breakfast. All Brianna wanted was coffee.

Brianna sat at a small table with a view of the courtyard, her fist on her chin.

A whirlwind month and what did she have to

show for it?

Likely she'd lose her job. Okay. That's not all bad. The farther from La Grande Bouche and that unscrupulous jerk Angus she could get, the happier she'd be. If nothing else, this humiliating fiasco taught her that much.

Her impetuously written story was so full of lies that she could never face anyone in Nocturne Falls again.

And after all this time, she'd finally connected with Jessica Callahan, though it wasn't exactly a movie-script reunion with all that talk of psychic abilities and falcon shifters.

She'd be amazed if Connor Ford even showed up this morning. If the tables were turned, what would she do? He'd left her with a promise that he'd help her find a way out of this.

Unless he turned back the clock long enough for her to retract that story, was there any other solution?

A plate of food appeared on the table next to her.

THE FALCON TAMES THE PSYCHIC

"I'm sorry, I'm waiting for someone." Brianna turned to see who insisted on sitting down, despite her explanation.

"They can sit somewhere else. Can you scoot the table a little? I need more room."

Connor? So, he did show.

After they repositioned the table, Connor chowed down on his overflowing plate.

As he slathered jam on a scone, he flashed a smile. "I hate to eat in front of you."

Sitting with him at breakfast seemed so natural. In another life, it might be after a long night of sweet lovemaking. With a falcon? Holy cats.

But he looked so human in his black t-shirt and jeans. She stared at a small spot of jam that clung to his lips. What fun it might be to kiss that away.

"Last night you said you might have a plan," she said.

Connor licked his lips, and the jam disappeared. "I didn't say I *might* have a plan. I said I *had* a plan."

He gestured to his plate. "You sure you don't

want part of this?"

She shook her head. "The plan?"

"Give me time to talk to my family. If you can get Angus out to my mother's house tomorrow night under the pretense of a party, I think we can convince him to pull the story."

That sounded a little shady.

Connor tore a piece of bacon lengthwise and stuffed half in his mouth. If these people were falcons, surely, they wouldn't dare swoop down on Angus and shred him to death like the bacon strip. Would they?

"You won't hurt him?" Brianna didn't like Angus, but she didn't want him physically harmed.

Connor pushed his plate away and leaned toward Brianna.

"What made you think we would?" He asked.

Oh, any number of reasons. A scary Hitchcock movie about the killer birds. No sleep last night.

"Guess it's stress," she said.

"Look, I need to go. I'd take you with me, but I need to handle this alone."

THE FALCON TAMES THE PSYCHIC

They agreed to meet later in the day for another trail run. Outside, a beautiful, crisp day. She had to get out of this funk. Perhaps another walk around town would help.

And this time she'd pay close attention. If there was truth to this supernatural stuff, she should be able to tell if she looked hard enough. Or asked the right questions.

Brianna looked along the street for the old truck. "Where'd you park?"

Connor tilted his head to the Porsche and laughed. "You're standing by it."

She turned to the cherry red convertible behind him.

"No. You're kidding. This is yours?"

Connor got in and started the engine. "Later we'll take her for a ride. Meet you at the trail head. Three o'clock." He waved and drove away.

If she didn't move soon, she'd become a pigeon roost. What part of Connor being a principal in Ford Financial Group had she forgotten?

"Does she mean that much to you?" Solange's unwavering gaze glued to the computer screen on her desk.

"It goes beyond that, Mother. It's about the town."

"This is a surprising reversal. I never knew you had that much love for Nocturne Falls."

"I didn't either." But Brianna's story would ruin everyone.

Solange rolled her captain's chair away and gestured to a seat next to the desk.

"Have you given further thought to our discussion about Atlanta? You need to get down there."

Great. Bargaining time.

If he wanted to come out of this with a win, he'd have to outsmart a master negotiator.

And fast and on the fly. Fly. What a glorious thought.

Now or never.

THE FALCON TAMES THE PSYCHIC

"I think there's a better plan for the company," he said.

Her eyes opened a quarter inch wider. "Better plan?"

"I think it's time to sell. Before the directors meet to block us, we exit and take away a fortune. You, Ryan and I are the majority owners. A call to the attorneys and we can get this in motion."

"Sell?" She slumped in her chair. "What are you saying? You can't mean this."

He didn't. But it worked to get her on the defense. Suddenly she wasn't the alpha falcon.

"Think about it, Mother. Then you wouldn't spend so much time staring at a computer screen, or worried sick about who was trying to screw us. Your golden years would be so much better."

"My golden years? Are you saying I'm old?"

Connor fought back a laugh. Pushing the vanity button worked.

"Of course not, Mother. But wouldn't you rather spend your days doing something other than staring at tabs on balance sheets?" Though Connor had no idea what the woman would do all day, besides harassing her sons. She'd never baked a cookie or planted a geranium in her life.

Solange returned to her computer and tapped the screen so hard, Connor braced it from falling.

"See these numbers? These spreadsheets? I love them. This is my life," she said.

Volley.

"See. That's what I mean. I'm not sure I'd do the position justice. I don't think I'll ever have that same joy as you once had."

"Once had? You think I've lost my passion? I'll show you passion. Right after we dispatch with this annoying tabloid thing, I'll march into that board room myself. I'll show them, and you and your brother, and anyone else who'll listen, that I still have what it takes."

"If you think you're up to it." Connor wished this was recorded for Ryan.

A deep breath filled Solange's chest. She held it a fraction of a second, then exhaled.

"Your brother and Jessica are in his studio

packing his equipment. I think it's time for a family meeting."

"I wouldn't put anything past those directors, Connor. Are you sure we aren't being played?" Ryan asked.

"What makes you think that?" Jess filled their coffee cups.

"Control," Solange said. "Jess, your experience with falcons is limited to the three of us in this room. After the boys' father died, we expanded to a worldwide corporation and we were forced to diversify the board."

Solange stirred cream into her cup in a slow circle. "Sadly, not all of us are ethical. There are those who would do anything to shame or humiliate the Ford family and force us out. This whole exposé might be a reverse scam. It may not have anything to do with Nocturne Falls."

"Maybe Brianna's sudden appearance might be part of their plan," Ryan said.

Connor pounded his fist on the table. "That's enough, both of you. It has nothing to do with the

FFG. Brianna Putnam is not a pawn of some takeover scheme. Hold up on the paranoia and keep these two things separate."

"I wish I could," Solange said.

"Look, if none of you will help, fine. I'll take care of this myself. Even though Brianna caused this giant cluster, she needs help. And this town doesn't deserve this story to get out."

"The man will be here tomorrow. I say we risk it," Ryan said.

"Mother, are you in?" Connor's gut wound so tight it growled.

"On one condition." Her smile pierced her stern countenance. "Atlanta."

"Damn." She was a patient falcon, through and through. While she waited for the right moment, she played him all along like a fine-tuned guitar, then pounced. At this point, there weren't a bucket of options. "I agree."

"Wonderful. Now, what time shall we expect your young lady friend and Mr. Angus whatever-his-name is?"

THE FALCON TAMES THE PSYCHIC

CHAPTER EIGHTEEN

Brianna felt like a bird on a wire facing a hurricane.

That's a laugh. Birds had sense enough to hunker down somewhere safe till a storm was over. Exactly what she wanted to do right now.

But she'd created this storm and she had to ride through it.

Connor sounded so confident as they had jogged along the trail together yesterday. 'It's all arranged,' he'd said. All she had to do was get Angus to the Ford home for a meet-and-greet to welcome the visiting celebrity to Nocturne Falls.

Celebrity? If that's what they wanted to call

him. Stinking sack of caca would be a better description.

With Connor, she felt this would turn out fine. Alone in her room and after another sleepless night, the niggling doubts returned.

Then, forty minutes ago, Angus called that he was almost there. He'd sounded like a slobbering, ravenous dog, hungry for a bloody piece of meat.

She paced the sidewalk watching every car drive by. Smiling face after smiling face. Happy go-lucky tourists.

The librarian drove past, waving out the window.

"Hey, Brianna. Come back by when you can. Found more info you might like," he said.

What a sweetheart. Wonder what kind of supernatural creature he really was?

A white sedan slowed to a stop at the curb.

Her stomach bounced to her throat. Angus.

Whatever Connor had planned better be good.

Angus Harper spent the whole time they were in the car on the phone, to Brianna's relief.

He didn't respect her any more than he did a paperclip. All he wanted was a story. Didn't matter how he got it or who got it. He didn't even acknowledge the crappy way he treated her on the phone two days ago.

She glanced at her bracelet. Though tempted, now would not be a good time to read his mind.

After ending the sixth call in a row, he turned to her. "Where is this place anyway?"

To tell the truth, she had no idea. She'd only met Connor in town, at the Carpe Diem, or at the falls.

"Your navigation screen says turn right in a quarter mile," she said.

She didn't know much about Connor. And thanks to her mucking everything up, she'd lost the chance to learn more. He'd drop her like a hot coal once this was over. Why wouldn't he?

Angus pulled to a stop at a locked gate. "Now what?"

THE FALCON TAMES THE PSYCHIC

Somehow Brianna had pictured a much smaller entrance. Maybe a wooden arm that would lift. Not this mammoth iron castle gate. "They told me to press the speaker button. Number 36."

In a moment, a woman's voice greeted them. Once Brianna announced who they were, the gate unlocked and opened.

Angus muttered something about gates in a Podunk town being overkill while Brianna stared at the houses.

Huge, elegant homes. Expansive, manicured yards.

This had to be part of Connor's game plan. He'd talked someone into hosting this pretend party.

After winding through the neighborhood, the GPS screen flashed that they'd arrived at the destination. Connor Ford had some mighty good friends.

Then it hit like a bomb. Ford Financial Group. The brothers were primaries. The Porsche. As smart as she was, why hadn't Brianna pieced this puzzle together before now?

"Well, you getting out or not?" Angus had opened her passenger door.

She hadn't noticed he'd even stopped the car.

Thank God it was Connor who answered the home's front door.

"Please join us in the living room," Connor said as he walked beside Brianna.

He slipped his arm around her shoulder and gave her a reassuring hug. She tried to smile but her lips were glued to her teeth.

She couldn't even blink her eyes as she stepped into the foyer.

This wasn't a home. It was a small-scale Versailles. Walls covered in framed paintings of pastoral gardens. Hallway tables held ornate porcelain vases.

Was the man in the dirty cap and grubby clothes she'd met in the driveway of the Carpe Diem a month ago, part of this?

No. This was a dream. She was sleep walking. Or, too much caffeine and not enough REM sleep. Big joke on her.

THE FALCON TAMES THE PSYCHIC

Here she was, a middle-class kid from Oregon standing in a million-dollar mansion. Connor Ford had his pick of women. That he'd shown any interest in her at all, even for the short time they'd had together, was a miracle.

When her eyes found Ryan and Jess, she calmed down an inch.

Red hair piled high, Jess was stunning in a black, sleeveless cocktail dress. Ryan wore a dark gray shirt, and black slacks.

She cut a glance to Connor, still with his arm around her. Maybe she should pinch herself. He was so incredibly handsome. For a falcon, that is.

Solange walked toward them and offered her hand to Brianna.

"At last, we meet." She held Brianna's hand as she glanced at Jess. "What an amazing resemblance she has to your grandmother."

Solange Ford was nothing like Brianna anticipated. Taller than Connor, she commanded the room in a way that seemed a bit overdone. A textbook foil for Angus Harper.

Solange gestured to the bar at one end of the room. "Please, everyone, help yourself. Sabrina will prepare any drink you wish."

A full bar and bartender?

Drinks in hand, Solange and Angus stood off to the side chatting, one-sided of course. Angus had the social graces of a rhino and never knew when to shut-up.

Solange nodded and smiled. The supreme hostess.

"Hanging in?" Connor whispered in Brianna's ear.

"Barely. I'm not sure what's going on," she said.

"When I give you the nod, make your way over to Jess. And Brianna, if it gets too intense, Sabrina will take you back to town. I'll understand."

He kissed the back of her hand, holding his warm lips long enough to make her wish they could find a room in this ginormous house where they might have privacy.

But leave? Nothing short of a nuclear blast

would get her out of this house now.

Connor continued holding her hand as his eyelids narrowed. "Remember, stay with Jess."

She smiled at him in an unsuccessful attempt to break through his steely stare. "I got it."

Whatever '*it*' was.

Ryan and Connor stood together behind the wingback chair where their mother had taken a seat. If they were dressed in period costumes, the trio would pass for a Victorian dynasty.

Something seemed odd. It was as though they were taking stage positions.

On his second martini, Angus sat across from them, still yammering.

Solange politely nodded as though she gave a rat's left foot about what Angus was saying.

Jess sidled over to Brianna and took her hand. What the heck? Wasn't this the same Jess who played the ice queen at the barbecue? Now she wanted to hold her long-lost cousin's hand?

"Have you ever seen him shift?" Jess whispered.

"What? Who?"

"Connor," Jess said.

"I saw him move closer to Ryan if that's what you mean."

Jess smiled and shook her head. "Stay close."

"So, Angus. About the story Brianna submitted. Are you still planning to publish it?" Solange asked.

"Hell, yes. Our readers believe anything we put out there. This one will reel in the bucks. Right up there with the alien baby stuff." He leaned forward in his chair, his forearms on his thighs, rolling his drink between his hands. "I'm sure you understand what I mean."

He looked around the room. "This hobgoblin town has worked out well for you. There's a sucker born every minute, they say."

Solange sat tall in her chair and cocked a glance at her sons. "We would concur with that."

Connor stared straight at Brianna and nodded. Jess's grip tightened.

"I knew it," Angus said through a malevolent laugh. "My kind of people."

THE FALCON TAMES THE PSYCHIC

"I doubt that." Solange gripped the chair arms. "Gentlemen, shall we?"

CHAPTER NINETEEN

First the glimmer.

Solange and her sons were enveloped by a dim gray-white light that quickly turned to LED bright.

Then a distant whirring like the sound of a thousand wings grew louder, filling the room to a deafening level.

Brianna covered her ears as she tried to focus on Connor's face that soon disappeared into an opaque shroud. She felt her cousin's hug around her waist tighten.

"Jess?" Only one word had the nerve to escape.

And then it ended. The room quieted. The shimmering lights disappeared.

THE FALCON TAMES THE PSYCHIC

So had Solange, Ryan, and Connor.

In their place were three very large Peregrine falcons perched on the chair.

"Come with me." Jess guided Brianna to an out of the way corner.

"Now, take some deep breaths." Jess put her hand on Brianna's back. "It helps."

Between gasps, Brianna formed a feeble question. "What was that?"

"When they shift as a group, it's quite a show," Jess said.

"It's true? Everything Connor said was true?"

"Judge for yourself. Look at your boss."

She'd never been this close to uncaged predators. Their beaks and talons were designed to capture and kill. Who or what would be their next victim?

Their appearance was spellbinding. To think each of these was a human being moments ago. The one that had been, or was, Connor was broad chested and had a slight turn to his head while he kept his eyes on her.

Remembering Angus was in the room, she turned her attention back to him.

Bloodless as a corpse, his face was a portrait painted in fear. Hot damn. Seeing this was worth her own cardiac failure.

Solange was the first to return to human form.

She dusted a few rogue feathers from her lap, then smiled at the falcons on either side. "Nice job, sons."

"Sabrina, please fix Angus a drink? I think he needs one," Solange said.

"What about Ryan and Connor," Brianna whispered to Jess.

"They're fine. And you?" Jess asked.

"I wish I knew." Brianna stretched her arms behind her back and gave one a pinch. Pain. Not dreaming. This was real.

Angus took a long drink from the cocktail Sabrina brought him. "Excellent show. How'd you pull that off? This has Las Vegas written all over it. Better than the old disappearing tiger act."

Solange exploded in a netherworld laugh that

rattled the ice in Angus's glass.

"You are in Nocturne Falls, my dear man." Solange steepled her fingers. "The magic of Halloween extends beyond the celebrations and town decorations. Through the beneficent grace of the Ellingham family, we, and others can live in a community that embraces us."

Solange cast a loving glance in the direction of Brianna and Jess, then continued.

"Our day-to-day lives are just like yours." Solange tipped her head toward Angus and cast a dark stare. "Perhaps not exactly like yours. But we run businesses, marry, raise children."

In an instant, Ryan reappeared in human form, and Jess walked to his side. Why didn't Connor shift?

"We hope you understand why we ask you not to publish Brianna's story," Ryan said.

Angus tossed back the rest of his drink.

"Are you kidding? This story will put La Grande Bouche on the map and sell a million copies. Where's that bartender? I need another drink."

Brianna's heart puddled at her feet. The plan had failed. Reasoning with this stubborn ox was hopeless.

She didn't know this family well, but they had jeopardized everything to help her. And Angus had thrown it right back in their face.

It was all her fault. Was there anything she could do? If she could only get inside his scrambled thoughts and find a thread of compassion.

Inside his thoughts?

She had to try. If she suffered later, so be it. Better she hurt from a headache than hurt an entire town. She slipped off the bracelet and tossed it on the sofa.

Noisy voices started immediately. Ryan. Jess. Solange. She pressed her fingers to her temples.

Come on, sort through them. She hadn't used this '*gift*' deliberately before. Get a firm picture of Angus. Tune into his channel.

So hard. So noisy. Her own thoughts crashed through.

THE FALCON TAMES THE PSYCHIC

'Photos. Get them to do it again. Right price.'

She'd hit.

'Need better writer. Who can I get? Blow this wide open. Everybody has a price. What's theirs?'

Brianna had enough. She marched up to Angus and wagged her finger in his face.

"This town and these people are not for sale." Blood throbbed in her temples. "How dare you think they have a price?"

"Who said they did?" Angus roared.

"You did, and you know it." Brianna tightened her fists. It would be so easy to pummel this liar. Would her arrest be worth it?

"Brianna." Connor's hands rested on her shoulders.

In her rage against Angus, she hadn't noticed that Connor had shifted back to human. He slipped the bracelet back on her arm.

"Enough, everyone," Solange announced. "Sabrina, we need you."

Brianna's head was still reeling, but did she just hear Solange order more drinks? Was she kidding?

"I suppose the next thing will be the bartender turning into a snake." Angus's chortle reignited Brianna's fuse.

Sabrina casually walked into the room and stood a few feet from Angus.

"And what do *you* have for us?" Angus asked.

Sabrina's answer came in a sweeping arc of her hand. Whatever Angus was about to say next, froze in the air as did his body.

Brianna cocked her head toward Angus, then walked around his chair, poking him several times. No reaction. No response.

"Is he dead?" She asked.

"Heavens, no," Sabrina said. "I cleared his memory of the falcon shift and anything said after that."

"He'll be in this state for about ten minutes. Enough time for you to send him a retraction email," Connor said.

"Where's the closest computer?" Brianna asked.

Connor took her into Solange's office and

signed on to the computer. Brianna had the email ready in three minutes. She read it aloud to Connor, who asked her to repeat the last two lines.

"You heard me. I resigned. How about this last line? And you can take the Bouche and shove it," she said.

"Maybe cut that part," Connor said.

She shrugged, deleted the line, then hit send. Relief poured over her like a rain shower.

She'd just freed her soul from brutal captivity. And it felt so good.

"Your family was wonderful," she said.

"You weren't bad yourself. Pulling that bracelet off was gutsy. I know how it affects you."

The unasked question danced around them. Even with her bracelet on, it was easy to read his thoughts.

"To be honest, I was scared," she said.

"So was I."

"I mean, about watching you. The whole shift thing."

"I know."

"What's it like to fly?"

"I love it. Ryan hates every bit of it."

"Jess seems to be fine with what Ryan is."

"She grew up in Nocturne Falls. She's lived with supernaturals most of her life. For her, for all of us, it's what kind of person you are inside that counts."

"Your mother made a lot of sense about living in a place where you are embraced and feel safe. I envy that," Brianna said.

"It could be your home," he said.

If only that were true.

With Angus still frozen like a side of beef on ice, everyone took their original positions.

The stage was set for the big thaw.

Though everyone else seemed casual and relaxed, Brianna thought she'd burst.

Angus's eyes blinked then his right foot tapped the floor. He was coming out of it. What would he be like? Raging as usual? Meek as a mouse.

THE FALCON TAMES THE PSYCHIC

Solange took a sip from her fresh drink. "So, that's Nocturne Falls, Angus. We're not very exciting. Just a little tourist town in the mountains."

Angus reached for his drink but seemed surprised that his glass was already empty. Sabrina stood off to the side with a wide Cheshire cat grin. Angus better keep his mouth shut. No telling what else this woman might do.

"Solange, I couldn't agree more. I've wasted enough of your and my time." He turned to Brianna. "If you want my advice, try fiction writing."

Brianna picked an imaginary piece of lint from her knee to keep from laughing in his face.

"I'll consider that," she said.

CHAPTER TWENTY

Brianna stood with Connor at the gate and watched the rental car's tail lights disappear into the night.

Angus Harper was gone. For good. Forever.

"How did she do it?" Brianna asked.

"Sabrina? She's a Draoi."

"A what?"

"She practices ancient magic. Sabrina came here three years ago, after she was banished from her hometown. As hard-nosed as my mother is, she empathizes with outcasts. Sabrina was in a tough spot, so Mother brought her into our home."

There was way more to this new world than

Brianna could process tonight, or perhaps in a lifetime.

"Well, one thing's certain. It seems Sabrina makes a darn good cocktail and I could use a drink," Brianna said.

Inside, Solange, Ryan, and Jess sat around the enormous dining room table, laughing and joking about their performance.

Brianna wasn't entirely sure she should intrude. If it hadn't been for her, none of this would have been necessary. And without Sabrina, it would have been a disaster.

"Ah, there you are." Solange rose from her chair.

Brianna's gut twisted into a chain of knots. She'd witnessed the power this family held. If they wanted her out of their lives, would they ask nicely, or blast her into the ether?

"Brianna and Jess, please come with me," Solange said.

The women exchanged surprised glances as Solange waited in the doorway. "Well, come on," she said.

Brianna wished there'd been time for that drink. But she was in no position to argue with the person who had helped end the La Grande Bouche disaster.

Except for the sound of their footsteps echoing off the walls, the walk down the long hall was painfully quiet.

They stopped in front of a glass door. A solarium? Why should this come as a surprise in this place?

It certainly was odd timing for Solange to show off her orchids, but Brianna would put on her best performance and say how beautiful they were.

Solange opened the door and beckoned them to enter. "I'll leave you now."

She had to be frigging kidding. From Jess's look, she had the same thought.

Jess and Brianna held hands and walked through the threshold until they stood alone among hanging ferns, caladiums, and assorted flowering plants.

Jess's face dripped from the humidity. "What's going on?" She whispered.

Brianna wiped a trail of sweat off her temple. "Hell, if I know."

"No need to swear."

Brianna's knees buckled to a near collapse. "Who was that?"

Someone stepped from the shadows. "My two precious granddaughters. Together."

"Nana?" Jess hesitated a moment, then ran toward the small woman who almost disappeared in Jess's embrace. "I can't believe this. It's you. Really you."

Brianna stood in shock. This tiny woman was her grandmother?

"Honey, come over here," the woman said.

Willing her feet to move, Brianna's steps matched the cadence of her thumping heartbeat.

Her father's mother. The person he'd warned her about, stood before Brianna with open arms.

"Are you really her?" How stupid that had to sound.

Brianna wanted this with all her heart and wanted to run away at the same time. Once in her grandmother's embrace, Brianna wished for time to stand still.

The woman smelled of vanilla and lavender. Her soft cheek was a bit wrinkled, but the strength in her arms belied her age.

Tears blurred Brianna's sight. "I don't know what to say."

Echo's laugh tickled Brianna's chest. "How about hello?"

Brianna and Jess sat on a wooden bench while Echo told them about her adventures in China, amending her descriptions with broad gestures. The woman was so adorable. How could her father hold anything against her?

Finally, Echo explained she didn't have much time to spend with them.

"Why'd you choose to come back today?" Jess asked.

"To let you know that I was okay. And to meet my dear Brianna. And to add my blessing to the wonderful men you've chosen to marry."

Brianna's back stiffened. Chosen to marry? "I think you're confused. Jess and Ryan are engaged. There's no man in my life."

"Honey, someday we'll have a long, long talk. When I know something, I know it. You most certainly have a man. And your life with him is going to be wonderful. And both of you are going to give me some fine great-grands."

Great grandkids? What was she talking about? Brianna had barely met Connor. Wasn't it a bit too soon to order a wedding cake?

"Now, I need to scoot, but I'll be back for your weddings. I promise."

"Nana, don't go yet. Please," Jess said.

Brianna wondered if things could get any weirder. Afraid they might, she tried to shut down her thoughts. As though that was possible. And as though Echo wouldn't hear them anyway.

If only she had her grandmother around to help with this psychic gift business. And maybe fill in the gaps about her father.

"Brianna, honey, there's so much catching up we have to do." Echo reached for Brianna's hands and gently held them in hers. "I'll be delighted to teach you everything I can when I come back. As for your father and me, well that will take a long time to sort out. He was so attached to his father. When we lost him…"

Echo's voice hitched, and Brianna wondered if she had unintentionally opened an old wound. This tiny woman suddenly appeared so frail.

"I'm stronger than I look, honey." The twinkle returned to Echo's eyes as she cleared her throat.

"Both of you girls need to hear this. I suppose I can stay a few more minutes." Echo wedged between Brianna and Jess on the bench and took each girl's hand and gave a squeeze.

"My husband, your grandfather, was killed in action in Viet Nam. It wasn't easy for me to raise two kids alone. We were so lucky to find this town.

My daughter's psychic gift appeared when she was eight. Just as yours did. But my son, your father, Brianna, was just like your grandfather. A normal human.

I tried to make him understand he was perfect just as he was, but my son wanted to be like the other kids. He had no psychic gift. No supernatural abilities at all. I didn't care. He was my little man. My rock. I still love him with my whole being.

But his resentment festered for years. He left here bitter, distrusting and angry. At Nocturne Falls. At his sister. And at me. When Jess's parents died, he wouldn't take Jess into his home. More of his misplaced denial of who we are."

Jess and Brianna exchanged wide-eyed glances. Echo's story left Brianna speechless. Painful as it was, she'd wanted the truth about her father. This had explained so much, but she was left with more questions that she dared to ask, yet.

"Now I need to go before the three of us melt into a pool of tears. I won't have that. We come from sturdy stock. We are strong and can conquer anything."

She gave each girl a kiss. "Ciao, my precious ones."

And then Echo was gone.

After several minutes in silence, Brianna turned to her cousin. "Is it me or do people keep coming and going around here?"

"It's how things roll," Jess said.

"Anyone for a nightcap?" Solange announced as Brianna and Jess returned to the dining room.

"Not for me. I'm going back to the Inn. I'm exhausted," Brianna said.

"We can give you a lift," Ryan said.

"Ah, I got that covered," Connor said.

Brianna felt the bloom of school-girl awkwardness flush up her neck.

On the ride, Connor kept the top down on the car. Brianna watched a shooting star graze the sky.

Somewhere out there her grandmother was practicing Tai Chi, several centuries in the past.

Inside the Ford mansion, a family of falcons had shifted before her eyes.

A woman cast a freezing spell on someone.

THE FALCON TAMES THE PSYCHIC

A prediction that she was going to produce great-grandchildren with Connor.

Her grandmother opened a door on her father's past.

All in all, a typical date night.

The Porsche whirred to a stop in front of the Inn. Without a word, they walked to the porch.

When they reached the first step, Connor asked, "So, what's next?"

Brianna took a deep breath and exhaled in a long sigh. "Next? I figure out the rest of my life." Now with her grandmother's story, she walked a high-wire between two worlds.

She interlaced her fingers and pressed her locked hands behind her back. "I suppose I'll go home to Portland." Which meant facing her father.

"You don't have to," Connor said.

Had he read her mind? No. He was a falcon. Not a psychic. Coincidence.

Connor ran his hands along Brianna's arms until she released her fists.

"I need to go to Atlanta. Family business.

Would you consider coming with me?" He asked.

The sweet sincerity in his gaze gave her happy chills. Her father had been wrong to leave here. And she would be right to stay.

"We've never been on a real date except when you took me to lunch." Jogging. Coffee. Site seeing. Stranding her on a mountain. And scaring Angus half to death didn't count in Brianna's book.

"Meaning what?" Connor asked.

"Meaning, I think Atlanta would be a beautiful place for a real dress-up date. Don't you?"

Connor gave Brianna's neck a light massage, electrifying every cell in her body.

"People might talk," he said.

She reached around and locked her thumbs in his waistband. "Meaning what?"

He leaned closer, pausing just before his lips met hers as their warm breath mingled. She knew in her heart that this moment would change their lives forever.

"Meaning this." His mouth covered hers and found her tongue.

THE FALCON TAMES THE PSYCHIC

His fingertips swirled around those goofy spots on her skull that made her lose all rational control.

After a lovely, languid moment lost in his embrace, a giggle rose from her belly and escaped into his mouth.

He broke the kiss, and his puzzled expression made her laugh even harder.

"What's wrong?" He asked.

"It tickles," she said.

"Huh?"

She reached under her shirt and into her bra, then retrieved the feather from the falls that she'd brought for good luck.

"This," she said. "Is it your habit to drop these everywhere? I'm not the kind of woman who goes around picking up after a man. Just want you to know that up front."

He lightly kissed her cheek. "Got it."

"And promise you'll give me a little notice next time you plan to shift?"

He nibbled down her neck. "Uh huh."

"And, will you please stop fooling around and

kiss me right?"

He ran his tongue up her chin and around her lips.

The man drove her mad. For more.

He gave her lower lip a soft bite, then tipped her chin toward him.

"One more thing." He kissed her nose. "Have I told you how much I love you?"

Moonlight glinted off the silver bracelet she held in her hand. "I already know."

"You better put that back on. Some of my thoughts should stay private," he said.

"Agreed. And for the record, I am madly and totally and *featherly* in love with you, Connor Ford."

"Featherly?"

"Just kiss me."

THE END

ABOUT CANDACE

Candace lives and writes on Florida's Gulf Coast where she practices yoga, Tai Chi, and takes long walks on the Pinellas Trail. Before venturing into full-time writing, she taught K-12 public schools. Later she taught in two community colleges and in a university. Her middle career was in health care.

Candace was hooked on genealogy the minute she discovered her ninth great-grandmother, Rebecca Towne Nurse was hanged as a witch in Salem, MA in 1692.

To learn more about Candace, visit her online:

www.CandaceColt.com
www.facebook.com/CandaceColtAuthor
www.pinterest.com/fortheluv2write
www.twitter.com/Candace_Colt

Special thanks to these amazing people:

Jax Cassidy
Wynter Daniels
Melanie Newton
and
Kristen Painter

64803157R00252

Made in the USA
Middletown, DE
18 February 2018